I0832519

The Episodes:

Episode 1: Hijo De Xavier or, What Happens in Los Volcanes!

Episode 2: The Horvitz Hour! (Üzchalcyon Enmity)

Episode 3: ZZZ (The Triple Zed Project)

Episode 4: The Phlea Circus

Episode 5: This Little Piggy

Episode 6: Fly Me To The Moon (WIP)

Episode 7: HATEBAKE (Üzchalcyon Enmity)

Episode 8: Customer Buttcheeks

- ACT I: WEEK 1
- ACT II: RIVALRY WEEK
- ACT III: NIGHT OF THE HIGH SCORES

Episode 9: When Is Now? BOOK I: Archimedes!

Episode 10: When Is Now? BOOK II: Recalcitrance!

www.inejiro.tokyo

The First Edition

This book is a work of fiction. All characters, places, incidents, and dialogue are the product of the author's imagination and are not to be construed as real, or if real, are used fictitiously. Any resemblance to any actual events, locales, or persons, either living or dead, is purely coincidental. So, there.

Cover Design by Patrick Francis Waters

www.inejiro.tokyo
www.luxarium.info

ISBN: 978-1-957174-03-7

Kalyanji-Mandeep
Published by Coffin & Crown LTD

Original Music at
soundcloud.com/deeproy

<u>*Amplify:*</u> [**am**-pl*uh*-fahy] (v) 1. To make larger, greater, or stronger.

In 2115 The UN takes notice of the inability of its member states to properly govern their people. Riots, protests, and political assassinations have led up to a catastrophic event in the 53rd state, the San Francisco Bay Area, which forced the UN to step in.

Now the war is over and countries loyal to their UN membership have recovered and are on the rise. This anthology tours the globe, giving readers insight into the bizarre goings-on now that 70% of the planet lives under one government.

Plant hybrids, masked gangsters, time travel, super science. All episodes in this series connect and shed light on each other.

For You

"One less mouth, one more day..."

...EPISODE 4

The Phlea Circus

Author's Note:

Hello. This book was written in a Japanese format known as Kishotenketsu. This format employs a four-act model, as opposed to the Western three-act model, and is meant to broadly display a suite of information.

Ki – Introductions: Meet the characters, the settings, and get a general idea of what may be occurring.

Sho – Deepening: Learn why things are the way they are and why they may unravel.

Ten – Complication: Things fall apart.

Ketsu – Resolution: The results of the complication and its effects on the deeper things that were previously introduced.

I chose this format as I feel it best frames the collection of data that survived the carnage and misanthropy just prior to the dawn of Our Amplified Earth.

-小泉稲次郎

Patrick Francis Waters

Ki

introductions

VIDEO COPYRIGHT 2114 US FEDGOV

!!!ABOVE TOP SECRET!!!

"Hi there! My name is Gaia Pany and I am here to introduce you to the eminent Warren G. Harding Federal Correctional facility here in gorgeous [LOCATION REDACTED]! Our virtual four-dimensional tour starts in the luscious gardens that line the Doctor's dorms. These gardens not only provide food, beauty, and narcoplants for the staff, but also a way to keep in touch with nature, to relax and zen out when the need arises.

Next, let's look into the dorms themselves! The Staff Quarters all have three bedrooms, two-and-a-half bathrooms and roomy balconies. Arranged in circular clusters, the dorms also serve as micro-communities with lush communal parks at the center of each village.

The Senior Doctors and other staff in the management echelon reside here, on Onogoroshima Island! TASC spared no expense in constructing a fully functional in-door paradise, set afloat on a crisp azure man-made sea. The Senior Staff will live in detached split-level housing. The model homes and housing layouts range from Victorian to American Classic, to Traditional Japanese. The weather's always perfect, the water always warm, and the privacy is unmatched!

From the Living Quadrant, it's just a quick driverless golf-cart ride over to the Athletics Facility! This cutting edge, multi-leveled complex sprawls across the grounds, taking up nearly as much space as the institution itself! Cricket pitches, soccer fields, baseball diamonds, a regulation PolyMatic football field, Amplified basketball courts, a full aquatic park, and even Jai-alai! While this facility is primarily for the staff's enjoyment, inmates will also be allowed to use certain athletic elements! (At their doctor's discretion of course!) *wink*

Just beyond the athletic grounds exists the powerful horn-of-plenty that keeps this facility fed! The 15-story agro-construct is completely autonomic and self-sustaining. Bots stand at the ready to harvest at a moment's notice, in addition to countless other duties, all monitored in the crown jewel of WGH, the Orbital Tower, affectionately nicknamed The Cyclops!

In the center of the main penitentiary construct stands the proud Tower. Guards, orderlies, and nurses all stand at the ready, eagerly observing inmates in their cells and on the grounds. The sphere placed neatly on top serves as the nerve center of the main lock-up. In addition, the hulking orb serves as the main generation point for the invisible ionic field that drapes over the facility proper!

Say, why don't we introduce one of our most exemplary guards, Viktor Tandy!

"Hi folks, I'm Viktor Tandy. I oversee the day-to-day guard operations here, and if you're lucky, you may get to watch me bowl the doctors right out of this facility on the Cricket Pitch!"

"Oh, Viktor!"

"Haha, why don't I take you inside the Cyclops' Keep on the top floor? Here, guards watch around the clock, making sure all the inmates behave 24/7. Not only can we monitor from here, but we can act too. Look out A spider!"

"Wow that was close Vik!"

"Scared ya didn't I? Well, there's no need to be scared! What you just saw was a *Spyder*. These golden bots swing from cell-cluster to cell-cluster acting as order-keepers on our behalf. See, if a fight breaks out in the north-western Green-psi cluster, we can just tell a Spyder to swing over, interfere with the brain waves of the psi, thus disabling him, bind him, and then return the offender to his cell. Beautiful."

"Wow, thank you very much for that informative piece. Viktor Tandy y'all!"

"Thank you, Gaia and thank you Mr. President."

"Isn't he just wonderful? Our final looky-loo will be at the penitentiary itself…

"The prison is divided up into Clusters:

Green for psionic offenders,

Red for thieves and gangsters.

Blue for violent offenders and murderers.

Yellow for 'white-collar' boys (not too many of them here).

Orange for the criminally insane!

The cells are pod-like. A bed, a toilet, a shelf and a small window. Clustered like grapes, they almost hang in bunches amongst the black steel and iron webbing that comprises the whole of WGH."

"Well, I sure do hope this video was informative and helpful! Enjoy the rest of your time here at Warren G Harding, have a blessed day!"

Map Key*

A. Airstrip
B. Warren G. Harding Complex
C. Cyclops Tower
D. Onogoroshima Island
E. Warden's Mansion
F. 1. Guards
   2. Nurses
   3. Assistant's Row
G. Cricket Pitch
H. Gymnasium
I. PolyMatic Football/Soccer Field
J. Swimming Pool
K. Kitchen Staff Quarters
L. Orderlies, Janitors, et al.
M. Airstrip Tower

*X indicates bamboo forest. Striped areas are designated Recreation Zones

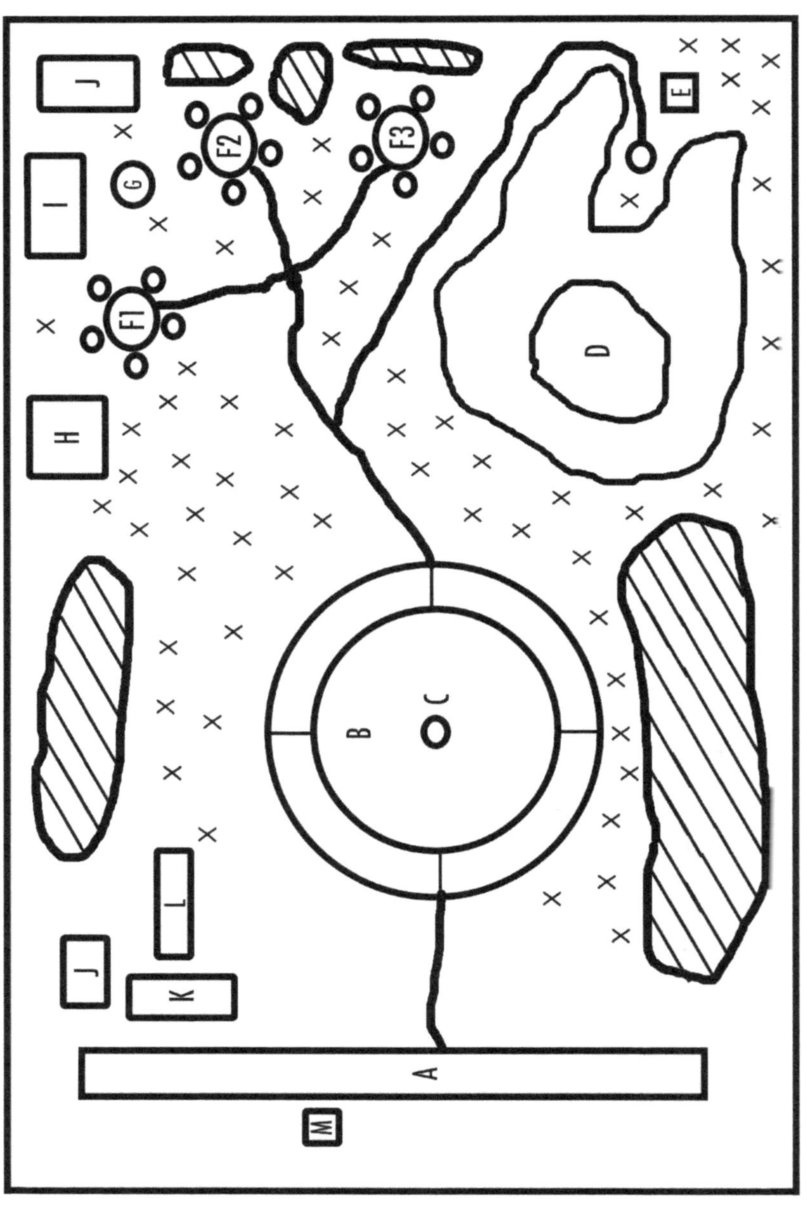
J
E
F2
F3
G
I
F1
D
H
C
B
L
J
K
A
M

30 Months Before Unity

San Leandro, California

Marlin Fevers woke to his alarm. His wife, Pepper, continued her slumber. Marlin rose from their great and cushy bed. He did some light stretching and threw on his pink robe, won at a block party, to go and feed his urban chickens.

He turned the TV on almost immediately after scurrying back inside. There was a Breaking News alert flashing on the bottom of the screen. Then again, his news channel of choice always had a bright red Breaking News alert on the bottom of the screen, just above the crawl.

Marlin ignored the call to attention. Instead of plopping down right there and absorbing whatever the news director felt was so pressing, Marin set to making his breakfast: six poached eggs, four pieces of bacon, two slices of toast, some baked beans, a roasted tomato, and some capers. He set all this on the table in front of the television, still ignoring the Breaking News. He next made coffee. Then he poured a glass of pear juice. Before he took his liquids over to join his solids, Marlin ingested his daily pill regimen.

His final ritual prior to breaking his overnight fast involved a whistle, two claps, and a rousing series of high-fives, all directed towards a signed photo of himself standing proudly alongside then-candidate Pickford-Saxby

De La Croix.

"I Pick PICK!" read the slogan on the green and gold banner behind the two oddly shaped men.

At last, Marlin Fevers sat down to breakfast.

He almost choked when he finally turned his attention to the screen.

"Breaking News folks, an oil rig near Svalbard has exploded. The drilling platform has sunk into the Arctic Ocean, and the spill is growing rapidly..."

The footage was horrific.

There were bodies floating in the sheen.

"This is bad..." Marlin said to himself. His wife was now snoring.

Several days later, the spill was declared "out of control" by Norwegian and Russian authorities. There was an appeal for suggestions and methods to handle and eventually stop the spill. Ships with booms did little to nothing. The oil was starting to enter the currents swirling around the Arctic.

Well after the call for assistance went out, a team of scientists from Beijing University appeared on the scene. They flew into the small landing strip outside the seed vault to much fanfare from the other assembled scientists. The August Professor Li Wu Hong took charge.

Professor Hong carried with him only one small item: a test tube filled with "the answer" to the oil in question. The Chinese government instructed the professor to wait until a flotilla they had prepared arrived.

The professor chose to ignore the order, citing the growing sheen.

Professor Li Wu Hong was ferried out to the coordinates of the former drilling platform. Here, from the dead center of the spill, did Professor Li Wu Hong invert, and then empty the contents of, his glass test tube.

For a long time, nothing happened.

The amassed scientists, technicians, geologists, oceanographers, chemists, physicists, climatologists, and diplomats all clung to their individual hopes and faiths.

The Chinese flotilla arrived.

Needless to say, they were not very happy that Professor Hong did not wait for them. Professor Hong went aboard the flagship, surrounded by guards and pageantry, and never came out.

In hour fifteen of nothing happening, an event began to unfold.

From the exact spot where Professor Hong had poured his test tube came a ring of clean ocean seven meters wide. Another hour later, the ring was one kilometer. An hour after that, the disk of clean ocean water encompassed the flotilla.

There was a microscopic rend in the hull of one of the Chinese ships. The location of the crack just happened to be in the area of the ship where bilge was pumped out. The new, clean, ocean water seeped in, mixed with the bilge, and was almost immediately pumped out.

Professor Hong had bred a new species of oil-eating bacteria. This bacterium was designed with a measure of "staying power", as their rate of consumption, in his opinion, was rather slow. He had grown this bacterium in the hopes of cleaning up gas station concrete tanks, construction messes, auto shop used oil, and he had forecasted its use in cleaning oil spills. He had never tested it outside of a very controlled environment, though.

The clean ocean water seeping into the hull of one of the destroyers began to clog the bilge pumps. One of these pumps, doing its best to be a diligent little machine, overheated and exploded. The explosion damaged a fuel line and converted the small rend into large one. A new sheen began to spread out across the now clean ocean water. Professor Hong's bacteria took to the new sheen with ease. In fact, it liked the processed diesel fuel so much, it swam up stream like a salmon and made its way into the massive fuel tanks. Within fifteen minutes the destroyer was dry and where the fuel had been there was now pinkish green webbing and growths like mold.

The admiral gave the order to pull anchor. The decision had been made to tow the fuel-poor destroyer back to China. The only problem was the gaping hole leaking bacteria freely into the ocean.

Professor Hong could not be reached for comment.

Three months after the disaster, dubbed The Chinese Arctic Catastrophe, Norway ran out of oil. Two more months after that, the entire North Sea was devoid of oil.

Nervousness set in around the world.

The destroyer that was towed back to China brought with it the virulent strain of bacteria created by

Professor Hong. Within weeks, all Northern China was oil barren.

OPEC called an emergency meeting.

Oil production was quadrupled. The excess oil was barreled and locked away in Top Secret locations. Oil prices were frozen, to stop the wild and strenuous market swings.

Then OPEC issued an official statement, formally placing the blame at the feet of China. It was their scientist who developed the bacteria. It was their scientist who failed to wait for the flotilla. It was their destroyer that brought the Oil Pest to China proper. From a world standpoint, the Russian drilling platform's poor maintenance record was a moot point. It was Red China that chose to punish the world's capitalistic leanings. It was Red China working against traditional democracy and free trade. It was Mao's sesquicentennial ideology that fueled the Chinese anti-capitalist actions.

Marlin Fevers, his wife Pepper, and the rest of the citizens' lives in the 53rd state of the San Francisco Bay area would never be the same.

There was a boycott of Chinese goods. China Towns across the country, and world, were protested and looted.

When the wave of anger and confusion passed, everyday people resumed their lives as best they could. Home grown Electric car sales skyrocketed, with precious metals coming from the rich northern mines of The

United Republic of Korea, recovered and restored by the South Korean government in 2103. The demand was almost too much. A new era of oil-free, China-free, innovation broke out in Silicon Valley.

OPEC locked the door on their hidden ocean of oil barrels and threw away the key.

Soy, hemp, and corn became the hottest commodities on the market. New plastics were introduced, and relief at last began to set in.

That is, until many of the old guard realized their position mirrored that of one William Randolf Hearst in the 1930's: either adapt to the new means of production, or dig in your heels and use the courts to bolster your current grasp. Hearst used his papers and influence to make hemp and its by-products illegal in 1937, rather than convert his timber holdings to industrial hemp. In the Present, the still-extant Rockefellers and other Old Money oil families channeled Hearst and did their utmost to stall the influx of new oil-mimicking botanical products, while ostensibly cheering the eventual return of classic petroleum products. One such method involved continuous visits a draws from a Rockefeller well on Easter Island. It was entirely untouched by the Pest, and very, very, deep. The family told all who asked that the oil they were pushing came from their seemingly dilatant reserves. This action tipped inflation, completely screwed up the PetroDollar and fiat money system, and ultimately resulted in the financial disaster known as The Crush.

The global economy ground to a halt.

The wealthy resumed hoarding their riches.

Taxes on the lower classes swelled.

Then came the Oil Riots.

During all of these events, The United Nations and their powerful Secretary General, Rutherford Yun-Ping, along with his smarmy and sanguine Undersecretary Hyram Jeffs, and kept a watchful, judgmental, eye on the world leaders and their incompetent handling of the situation at hand…

3 Months Before Unity

Los Angeles, California

Maximo Bluthe was the current Mayor of the city of Los Angeles. As he sat down to breakfast, he noticed before him on the table was his favorite morning meal: Korean Jook with all the trimmings, three glasses, one of local orange juice, one of lapsang souchong tea, and one of Amplified Botulin, a new health product, fresh from the TASC lab at UCLA. For dessert he would enjoy a frozen chocolate covered banana, his favorite.

"Uh, T-Tammy, Tammy darling?" he groped for his holopad. He pulled it from his wet-with-sweat pocket and set it on the table. "Oh, Tammy sweetheart, I need you, won't you come out?"

A kinky-haired blonde appeared on the holopad. "Yes, Mayor?"

"Tammy, what's my schedule for today look like? You, I hope." He winked and smiled in between shoveling hot jook into his mouth.

"Hmm hmmm," she sighed at his tepid advance. "Well you do have that meeting with the Keanu Society at lunch, and in the afternoon it's shotgun fishing with that nice old clone-gentleman from those old films."

"Stallone? Or Statham?"

"I believe it's Mr. Statham, sir."

"Very well, Tammy, thank you, don't go too far

sweet cheeks." Another wink, another fistful of jook.

"Attention May-ore Blu-th-é, stop vat ever it iz you are doin-k and giving me *all* ze money." A voice from behind said.

Maximo Bluthe slowly put down his utensils and stood. He wiped his face and greeted a Russian national, who was fumbling with an elaborate-looking device that smacked of Super Science.

"Say, whatcha got there pal?" He was nervous, but poised. His napkin fluttered from his shirt collar. The sun gleamed off his pneumatic robin's-egg-blue suit. The suit automatically changed to a pattern that Bluthe hated.

"Attention May-ore Blu-th-é, stop vat ever it iz you are doin-k and giving me *all* ze money." The man was a bit spastic and kept swatting at something Maximo couldn't see.

"H-hey hey now listen friend, there's no money here." Hands extended, palms open, he moved forward and off of the stone veranda of the Mayor's mansion and gingerly stepped a quivering slipper onto the TASC Amplified grass. This brave gesture let the Mayor's personal Praetorian know that things weren't quite right. Bluthe was terrified of grass, a fact his guard was very much aware of.

A swarm of camera-bearing scanbots sat unnoticed on several shrubs and topiaries in the vast yard. One by one they took flight and created a field large enough to project an image back to the Praetorian Hut and its chief, Gaius Aurelius.

"We move on this *now*, I want that Rooskie dead." No sooner had the words left his mouth were there three

Japanese men in white, orange, and green coveralls standing in his midst. The man wearing a badge, that displayed both “魔裟斗” and “Bill” as his name, extended a letter hand-signed by President De La Croix and Vice President Cairns. This deviant, this selfish, this pinko freedom-hating-borscht-worshipper was property of the US government and was to be handed over alive, intact and promptly, without argument or Gaius and his family would be constituted enemies of the state, treasonous in their aiding a foreign enemy to escape the hand of the mighty corporation that is the United States.

Gaius let out a gruff, annoyed sigh and sent a creeper to grab him before the Super Science device he brandished engaged and erased this portion of the county.

Once inside the blob-like creeper, it was revealed his name was Pyotor Fyordorovich from Chechnya. A nuclear physicist turned black market arms maker. The letter Gaius had been handed went on to say that Pyotor was wanted in Astana for supposedly meeting with the Russian Finance Minister. He had discussed the proper rules and etiquette to use when purchasing pleasure bots (code for underage slaves) on Australia’s Gold Coast. He was to immediately be sent north to the 53rd state for intake into a newly renovated, and heretofore unknown to Gaius, prison facility.

‘Bill’ gave a simple and wan smile as the transporter ascended into the air, away from the glimmering LA Hills.

2 Months Before Unity

Oakley, Kansas

"Those eggs are *huge!*"

"Now didn't I tell ya he'd say that!"

"Alright alright, you sure did, here's your damned G$5," the trucker unfolded his mighty thick wallet and peeled off a Lincoln for the diner's needlessly buxom waitress, Pauline.

"Hey Cookie, you know what this is?" Pauline waved the bill at the cook who was knee deep in orders for ostrich eggs. "This here is five dollars for knowin' what's what!"

"You go girl!" The cook called from amidst his sea of egg shells and hollandaise.

The patron who initially remarked in reaction to his meal dug in and filled his face with albumin.

The diner door opened, causing the familiar bell to ding.

"Why hello there stranger, how many?" Pauline caught the bearded man shortly after entry.

The man handed Pauline a note.

"Cat got yer tongue? I'm just joshin' with yah sweetie, that's my way! Say, what ya got there?"

Pauline went from a spritely smile to a face of sheer terror.

"Mick! We got one! Mick! He's a Darwin!"

Mick, the cook, reached for his shotgun.

The eggy trucker remained in his original position.

The bearded man wore a look of panic in his eyes, but the giant white false beard made it look like one of derangement.

"Sir, I'm going to need you to back out from the diner, now," Mick had a bead on the beard and was slowly emerging from the kitchen.

"Please to read note!" The beard said in a muffled squawk.

A sudden twinge of pain struck the bearded man. He doubled over, clutching his stomach.

"Don't do nothin' stupid now!" Mick barked.

"The pain… my stomach…"

"Oh my god!" Pauline looked outside and noticed the dead truckers at the fuel pumps. "He killed those men!"

Mick cocked the shotgun, but before he could fire, a team of Amplified Police dropped their safety net over the diner. The front windows blew out and a bolo flew in, binding the false-bearded invader.

Officers flooded the restaurant and relieved Mick of his weapon.

"Scan him," Officer Moises Mbono took charge. He stepped over to the heap-of-a-man wearing a false beard, doing his best with bound arms to clutch at his stomach. Next to the commanding officer was a short Japanese man in a white, orange, and green jumpsuit. His name badge read both "見附" and "Jeff". 'Jeff' never said a word, but instead handed out small pieces of paper to anyone who wished to address him. One such paper identified the beard-wearer as a Belarusian named Alyosha. He was wanted in connection with a Dark Net website offering hitman and prostitution services for cruise ships.

Another officer came forward and waved a detection wand over the quivering human.

"It's another one, live and ticking in his abdomen."

"Deploy the creeper and get him out of here."

"Sir, I say, sir? What's going to happen to him?" Pauline was awash with curiosity.

"That's classified, ma'am. Just know that he wont be bothering you anymore."

"But he did kill those men at the pumps though, right?"

"Correct. He will be charged with their murder."

"What about that… that *beard* he's got *glued* on, can we see his real face?"

"These cultists are dangerous ma'am, very dangerous. We don't know if he has that bomb in his stomach rigged to blow if we touch it."

"Oh my gawd…"

"Yeah, this is pretty serious."

"Well, I'm thankful you and your officers got here so quickly, it's like you knew he would be here," Pauline laughed and wiped her forehead.

"Almost, huh?"

Back inside, the eggy trucker who lost the bet finished his plate and waited in silence for Pauline to get back. His coffee needed a refill.

85 Days Before Unity

From the desk of UN Secretary General
*** Rutherford Yun-Ping ***

17 April 2115

To Pickford-Saxby De La Croix, President of the United States of America,

As you well know, the situations you are dealing with grow more worrisome each day. The international community has valid concerns. As your job is to first be conscious of the American people, my job is to first be conscious of the world at-large.

My chief concerns are as follows:

- The sharp rise of the Cult of Charles Darwin, and their attacks on the global community.
- The Chinese aggression on oil reserves.
- The actions taken by the Rockefeller, Astor, and Marriott families.
- Your insistence of using UNESCO monies for renovations on Alcatraz Island.
- The line items in your most recent UN supplementary budget, again requesting more humanitarian monies for unusual things like "Ambassador amenities" and "Ambassador

necessities," none of which have been approved by any committee.

Mr. President, while the Chinese situation is indeed pressing, due in large part to its economic implications, the activities of the cult surrounding Charles Darwin need to be addressed, openly and with force. The attack in your Nashville, Tennessee is what first comes to my mind. That incident caught the entire planet's attention. Now, new cells are appearing across Europe and Oceania. Their propaganda is potent and effective. Their slogan, "one less mouth, one more day," is being tagged in slums and university dorm rooms alike. Just yesterday, in Buenos Aires, an entire evolutionary biology underclass committed suicide while wearing great white beards. They had all carved the slogan into their forearms. This nihilistic doomsday religion needs to be eradicated. If you continue with your proposed course of inaction, we will be forced to sanction the United States.

On China, the consumption rate grows every day. Your own strategic reserves are getting low. The charade we're putting on with the aforementioned wealthy families will come to a head. Beijing refutes any and all claims made against it. My sources tell me there is indeed more to this situation than you and OPEC are sharing with the rest of the world. The firm denial of the Chinese is not falling on deaf ears.

The usage of UNESCO funds to "reinvigorate" the island of Alcatraz was at first well-received. The parking of a Trident D-5 Class submarine as a power source was initially hailed as conscientious. However, your constant request for funding has raised the suspicion of several other UN member-states. Mr. President, why does the decrepit museum need so much funding?

In regards to the line items labeled "Ambassador amenities" and "Ambassador necessities", such are the items that have thus far been requested: couriers, logistics, theater costumes, exorbitant pharmaceutical costs, and many, many other questionable items. Mr. President, could you please elaborate for the need of such expenses?

Going forward, the world is at a tipping point. We need oil, we need an answer for the Pest, we need an end to religious fervor, we need the United States to lead, not leach.

I look forward to our meeting on 21 July.

Give your wife, Diamond, my best.

In Solidarity,

潤平盧瑟福

Rutherford Yun-Ping

From the desk of the President of the United States of America

20 April 2115

Dear Mr. Secretary General,

I have read your letter, and fully understand your concerns. The episode in Nashville was an unfortunate one, as were the other high-profile Darwinist suicide attacks in Los Angeles, Oakley, and New Haven. We are aware of their leader, Alfred Russel Wallace II, however, we are not aware of his location. The cult grows with each setting of the sun. Clearly, Mr. Secretary, the adherents share our vision of potential despair given the current world conditions.

The situation caused by China is dire. Every day, another handful of our wells goes bust. Offshore drilling is yielding the same results. The Pest bacteria is rapidly spreading around the globe, and still Beijing does nothing. It is high-time China answers for their actions in turning the Pest loose on our oil-hungry planet. Perhaps sanctions, or even a full censure is necessary. Ambassador's Iyer and Da Silva assure me they are ready to fill-in any trade gaps created by the excision of the Chinese from the global economy. The United States in committed to a secure and assured global financial system.

The Rockefellers, et al., are American citizens, and are allowed to act as the Constitution defines.

Alcatraz is on American soil, and therefore subject to my direct oversight. There will be nothing further said on this matter.

The United States reserves its right to operational secrecy, as needed, for state security. With all due respect, the paper tiger you represent has no direct jurisdiction over our sovereignty.

Mr. Secretary, I hope this letter and the rest of your day finds you well. Diamond says hello.

In Solidarity,

Pickford De La Croix, President of The United States.

TO: VP@fed.gov
FROM: POTUS@fed.gov

SUBJECT: Flowers in the White House

MESSAGE: Hey Butch, when will a new bouquet of roses be brought in? My nerves are acting up again. UN Sec Ping is on my ass again about Alcatraz. When you can, get that I-Tie Benvolio on the horn and tell him to call me.

Yours,

Pick

TO: POTUS@fed.gov
FROM: VP@fed.gov

SUBJECT: RE: Flowers in the White House

MESSAGE: Hey Pick, the new roses will be in tonight.

Tell Ping to back off. My flight is tomorrow morning at 1000am and I'll be touching down at 1500pm.

I'll have Claudio call you after the flowers arrive.

Yours,
Butch

Dear Diamond,

My dearest Diamond, my post precious Gem. Oh, how I've missed your soft skin. The way you smell after a day conducting business... your natural scent excites and restores me!

After my plane lands at 1300pm, I'll have my driver take me straight to you. Please, keep yourself unwashed and in expectation!

The hours and days we've spent together...

Every moment away from you is torture! Pickford be damned, I need your body!

Remember, 1330pm, at our usual spot, I'll be freshly showered, and you hot and fecund!

Love,

Butchy

Dear Butchy,

Why hello there, my sweet little Butchy-boy!

I haven't worn deodorant for nearly a fortnight! Pick is thoroughly displeased and hasn't touched me since!

I'm all yours Butchy-boy!

When you arrive at our usual spot, 'll be flayed and splayed, eager for your clean hands to manipulate and devour my unbathed femininity.

Pickford be damned!

Love,

Diamond

Dear Chizzy,

Hey, you!

Butch doesn't suspect a thing! When you first told me you are the reincarnation of Napoleon Bonaparte and asked me to stop bathing, I thought we were cooked! Done for! Found out! What a twist that Butch thinks the same thing! After I prodded him into lusting after my ripe essence of course...

When can I feel your scepter in my garden again?

Oh Chizzy wizzy! My heart beats for you! We will flee, one day, together. That day is always on my mind. Our first State Visit to Canada was everything you said it would be! I can see our little cabin now, outside Medicine Hat, where no one can touch us!

I'm drunk on YOU my little Chizzy wizzy...

Love,
D.D.

Dear Di,

Hello my pet!

I, too, can't wait for our cabin in Medicine Hat.

I think of you at all times, when I'm on the floor, when I'm arguing a bill, when I'm eating, oh my sweet Di!

We need to change our dead-drop location. I think Pick or Butch is getting wise to us!

It's ok my Di. They'll never come between us!

Continue servicing Butch as needed, that way we can be ourselves as often as we like, and we'll throw him off our trail!

Oh my pet, my sweet peony, my lovely Di!

Your scent still lingers on my corpus...

Love,

Chizzy Wizzy

P.S. I have somewhere I need to be for a while. I'll send for you when it's safe...

The Personal Diary of President Pickford-Saxby De La Croix

20.April.2115

Replied to UNSEC Ping today. Oil prices spiked. Again. The Pest made it to the Alaskan oil reserves. Those are gone. 200 killed in riots in Chicago alone. Diamond is cheating on me, again. No idea with who, this time. Butch is almost back. Starting to feel addicted to lorazepam. Dividends from hemp holdings are growing. Hit on new intern today. She blushed and met me in the Solarium. She was black. She was wonderful. Don't know her name. Really miss having Butch around.

22.April.2115

Definitely addicted to lorazepam. Intern's name is Jennifer. We've had each other daily. Diamond stopped bathing regularly. Maybe she's depressed? She won't speak to me. Butch is back. Butch is happy to be back. Very happy. UNSEC Ping hasn't replied to my reply. Project Phlea Circus is moving along perfectly. Funds are filling the secret coffers. Payouts and hush money coming soon! That should shut Ping up. The Pest persists. The Chinese refuse to tell me when this whole 'Oil Pest' farce is to stop. Can't keep the lie going forever...

25 April 2115

Had the dream again. Mexican wrestling zombies, a pig stuffed with money, sugar sculptures, a gorilla named after Taft, and a giant crab. Butch says let it go. Diamond says the same.

28 April 2115

Alcatraz is going to be powered by a nuclear sub. More Japanese doctors to deal with. Will have to keep a tight leash on number of foreign prisoners let in. I think Darwin really was a cult leader. Thank God for that serial number...

THE TOKYO DAILY WORKER

2115 April 30

OIL PEST HERE TO STAY

Yersenia Pestis Olium, or The Oil Pest as you and I know it, is here to stay, this coming from the mouths of leading Geological and Pathological scientists.

The Oil Pest showed up shortly after the Svaalbard Oil Accident nearly two years ago, wherein an off-shore rig exploded and collapsed into the Artic Ocean. China, claiming sovereignty over the affected area, was the first to act, unleashing a new and un-tested method of oil cleanup.

Dr. Li Wu Hong is seen in the picture below famously pouring the 'single vial' of Oil Pest directly into the sheen. At first, everyone was pleased with the result. The oil vanished right before the eyes of all present. However, shortly after, it was discovered that the bacterium had followed the sheen down into the water and into the earth, tapping into the deep oil pit initially reached by the drilling platform.

From there the Oil Pest spread to other subterranean oil deposits, aggressively depleting the world's reserves.

The most recent analysis has yielded grave results. What

follows is a quote from Professor Ishant Kohli of Hyderabad University:

"Our research and data shows a total permeation of the planet's oil table. In short, the Oil Pest is everywhere, and it's going to stay there…"

Regardless of the outlook, diligent scientists remain hard at work, searching for a cure.

To: Hirasawa.K@tasc.co.jp
From: Endo.Y@tasc.co.jp

Subject: Timeliness

Message:

Kenji,

I've noticed several inconsistencies on your time sheets. You are marking down ten full hours of work, but our review of security camera footage shows you on site for less than nine hours. You are aware of our policy, and have personally requested to work ten hour shifts. What are you really doing with your time? Please turn over records from your digital secretary to HR before the week's end.

As you know, our new project is packed and ready to commence. The facility is nearing completion, and staff relocation efforts are under way. Please make sure you have all necessary items in place.

We will discuss matters further over lunch.

Sincerely,
Yoshida Endo
Lead Scientist
Takashinden Applied Sciences Corp.
4 Chome-21-5 Jingumae
Tokyo, Japan

To: Endo.Y@tasc.co.jp
From: Hirasawa.K@task.co.jp

Subject: RE: Timeliness

Message:

Dr. Yoshida,

I look forward to our lunch meeting.

Going forward, I will ensure my ten-hour commitment is met. I apologize for any misunderstandings or inconvenience my behavior may have caused.

I will send Collette's records over to HR after this email.

I have my checklist and it is nearly complete.

See you at lunch.

Sincerely,
Hirasawa Kenji
Associate Scientist
Takashinden Applied Sciences Corp.
4 Chome-21-5 Jingumae
Tokyo, Japan

Sho

deepening

8 Months Before Unity

[LOCATION REDACTED]

The snow covered hills and stolid winter sun offset the tremendous, encompassing canvas construct that sat nestled on a cleared out glen overlooking a white and restful valley. The thick canvas structure was wearing two hats; serving as a hotel and as a meeting hall for several very well-informed members of the Federal Government (sans POTUS, who was hot on the campaign trail), the Japanese Government, and the board of directors tasked with steering the financial interests of Takashinden Applied Sciences Corporation.

Each dignitary, as they had been classified, was woken at 0730am. A shower and a filling breakfast was provided, as well as freshly cleaned and pressed clothing. Once through with their various morning rituals, the dignitaries were guided to the Grand Hall. Here, a portion of the great Bedouin tent was peeled back to allow the sunlight in and onto those getting settled. The light was warm and perfectly set the mood for what was about to commence.

At the far end of the tented hall was a simple, but heavily decorated, stage and viewing screen.

The group now settled into their seats and onto their pillows. The canvas roof sealed itself and a projector clicked on. The gentle whir at the rear of the concourse was the only sound for several seconds.

"Hi there! My name is Gaia Pany and I am here to introduce you to the eminent Warren G. Harding Federal Correctional facility here in gorgeous [LOCATION REDACTED]*! Our virtual four-dimensional tour starts in the luscious gardens that line the Doctor's dorms. These gardens not only provide food, beauty, and narcoplants for the staff, but also a way to keep in touch with nature, to relax and zen out when the need arises.*

Several other projectors around the meeting hall now clicked on and began to display their vital pieces of the 4D experience. This went largely unnoticed as most of the dignitaries, being men, were entranced by the underdressed, bouncing Gaia Pany narrating the video.

"Next, let's look into the dorms themselves! The Staff Quarters all have three bedrooms, two-and-a-half bathrooms and roomy balconies. Arranged in circular clusters, the dorms also serve as micro-communities with lush communal parks at the center of each village.

"The Senior Doctors and other staff in the management echelon reside here, in Onogoroshima Island! TASC spared no expense in constructing a fully functional in-door paradise, set afloat on a crisp azure man-made sea. The Senior Staff will live in detached split-level housing. The model homes and housing layouts range from Victorian to American Classic, to Traditional Japanese. The weather's always perfect, the water always warm, and the privacy is unmatched!

"From the Living Quadrant, it's just a quick driverless golf-cart ride over to the Athletics Facility! This cutting edge, multi-leveled complex sprawls across the grounds, taking up nearly as much space

as the institution itself! Cricket pitches, soccer fields, baseball diamonds, a regulation PolyMatic football field, Amplified basketball courts, a full aquatic park, and even Jai-alai! While this facility is primarily for the staff's enjoyment, inmates will also be allowed to use certain athletic elements! (At their doctor's discretion of course!)

She winked at the camera, sending a wave of endorphins through the tent.

"Just beyond the athletic grounds exists the powerful horn-of-plenty that keeps this facility fed! The 15-story agro-construct is completely autonomic and self-sustaining. Bots stand at the ready to harvest at a moment's notice, in addition to countless other duties, all monitored in the crown jewel of WGH, the Orbital Tower, affectionately nicknamed The Cyclops!

The floating camera swooped around and started at the ground floor before zooming up to the top of the tower.

"In the center of the main penitentiary construct stands the proud Tower. Guards, orderlies, and nurses all stand at the ready, eagerly observing inmates in their cells and on the grounds. The sphere placed neatly on top serves as the nerve center of the main lock-up. In addition, the hulking orb serves as the main generation point for the invisible ionic field that drapes over the facility proper!

"Say, why don't introduce one of our most exemplary guards, Viktor Tandy!

A tall, curly white-haired man with piercing blue eyes smiled and flashed his perfect teeth at the camera.

"Hi folks, I'm Viktor Tandy. I oversee the day-to-day guard operations here, and if you're lucky, you may get to watch me bowl the doctors right out of this facility on the Cricket Pitch!"

"Oh, Viktor!"

"Haha, why don't I take you inside the Cyclops' Keep on the top floor? Here, guards watch around the clock, making sure all the inmates behave 24/7. Not only can we monitor from here, but we can act too. Look out! A spider!"

A robot with eight legs lunged past the camera. It was the size of a refrigerator and bright yellow. It was covered in camera lenses like a shoggoth has eyes and it bounded effortlessly between the ornate girders.

"Wow that was close Vik!"

"Scared ya didn't I? Well, there's no need to be scared! What you just saw was a Spyder. These golden bots swing from cell-cluster to cell-cluster acting as order-keepers on our behalf. See, if a fight breaks out in the north-western Green-psi cluster, we can just tell a Spyder to swing over, interfere with the brain waves of the psi, thus disabling him, bind him, and then return the offender to his cell. Beautiful."

A short clip of CGI inmates being wrangled by a Spyder gave a dramatic depiction of the events described.

"Wow, thank you very much for that informative piece. Viktor Tandy y'all!"

"Thank you, Gaia And thank you Mr. President."

"Isn't he just wonderful? Our final looky-loo will be at the penitentiary itself…

For each section, the video highlighted the wings of the prison as if they were decks on a cruise ship.

"The prison is divided up into Clusters:

Green *for psionic offenders,*

Red *for thieves and gangsters.*

Blue *for violent offenders and murderers.*

Yellow *for 'white-collar' boys (not too many of them here).*

Orange *for the criminally insane!*

"The cells are pod-like. A bed, a toilet, a shelf and a small window. Clustered like grapes, they almost hang in bunches amongst the black steel and iron webbing that comprises the whole of WGH."

The floating camera swung around to share the typically inmate dwelling.

"Well, I sure do hope this video was informative and helpful! Enjoy the rest of your time here at Warren G Harding, have a blessed day!"

Gaia Pany smiled and displayed her gleaming opalescent teeth. She then waved and waggled her large, burgeoning, breasts as the scene faded to black.

The projectors all clicked off, and soft chamber music began to play at a low volume.

"Ladies and gentlemen, as newly appointed Secretary of Incarceration, allow me to welcome you to Warren G. Harding Prison, tucked away here in the plains land of **[LOCATION REDACTED]**" Mansfield 'Butch' Cairns stretched his arms wider than his smile and nodded as the Japanese translator geishas surreptitiously informed the assembled dignitaries. He stood tall on the stage at the end of the tented meeting area. He was wearing a traditional black formal kimono, and was flanked by stout palms, lavish carpets and pillows, and several ornate kimonos on standing racks, laid out to display their radiant beauty.

The moniker for the operation as a whole, Operation Flea Circus, was a result of the final negotiations and preparations for this bit of Make-Work that was to serve as an economic dynamo. Inspired by the likes of the Meixi Lake development near Changsha in

China, Butch Cairns asked Dr. Yoshida Endo to nominate his powerful conglomerate as the sole contributor. He informed the doctor that America was choosing to opt for Fiscal Stimulus over direct Monetary Stimulus. His logic rested on the tech boom of the late 2000's that resulted in hundreds of "Unicorn Start Up" companies: coding companies that didn't really make anything but nonetheless found themselves worth billions on paper as a direct result of Federal monetary stimulus. These companies stood on the stimulus funds themselves, not windfalls of new profit. In addition, they were all hemorrhaging money in an effort to keep up the appearance or pretense of their unsubstantiated value. The bubble grew. Then the bubble popped. Cairns realized that the Federal Government had absolutely no control over what sectors would boom and how after direct monetary stimulus. Thus the decision was made to put on the elaborate Make-Work show that would come to be called Operation Flea Circus.

The only condition that TASC was required to adhere to involved the design, implementation, and maintenance of a flawless false reality.

The false reality would keep the prisoners unaware of the deeper situation, thus making them more readily compliant to any adjustments made inside while being completely cutoff from their various contacts on the outside. Endo and the TASC board readily agreed.

Then-Candidate De La Croix (really Butch Cairns, and largely without De La Croix's knowledge) had a stipulation of his own in that Takashinden Applied Sciences Corp (TASC) was to supply the security force in addition to what they had dubbed 'Amplified Reality' *at no cost* to the US Government. The soon-to-be President (Butch Cairns acting as De La Croix's representative) promptly agreed to TASC and their methods. Not just because the Crush had been much worse than anticipated, but in addition to his favorite tobacco, TASC also was the true source of funding for De La Croix's largest Super PAC, via Butch Cairns and his litany of shell corporations. One hand washes the other, which is ultimately washing itself.

Several moments after the four-dimensional experience had ended, the canvas enveloping the crowd of dignitaries was suddenly pulled away. The large group of mostly men were now greeted by a stunning view overlooking the entire facility, completely finished.

It was all there: the athletics complex, the bubble-like dorms, the agro tower, the facility itself, and out of the middle, like a lighthouse in a storm of architectural prowess, stood the imposing Cyclops Tower and its Keep. TASC had moved in *swiftly*. The buildings were a sparkling opalescent white with orange accents. Blinding green foliage almost overran the dorm and lab areas. The dorms as a whole held 50 scientists, 50 doctors, 100 nurses, 100 guards, their families, 200 dogs, 100 pneumonic snakes and many other facilities and items.

The main prisoner residence was the gem of the entire operation. The central housing structure was a giant bird's nest of crisscrossed black iron and steel, the Cyclops Tower being placed neatly in the center. The cell pod clusters looked like eggs expertly woven into the complex metal netting encompassing the facility as a whole. An ionic field was created to keep out the elements. When one stood within the construct, proper positioning would enable one to see right through the network of sharply angled girders. However, the precise positioning of the girders themselves were more than enough of a deterrent to keep the prisoners in their places, while giving the illusion of openness.

Several black helicopters appeared on the horizon. Landing within walking distance of the canvas structure, men in tuxedos dismounted from the flying machines and beckoned the dignitaries. Each helicopter was filled with self-important people, then lifted once more back into to the air, shuttling the VIPs down into the valley, to the facility.

Now standing outside the gates of the complex, the dignitaries sipped champagne and put in their orders for specific narcoplants to be brought to their respective rooms after the exhausting tour was over. Presently, several driverless transports, people-mover-like in their appearance, coasted up to meet them. Once inside, the large group was taken in successive waves through the interior of the facility itself.

The dignitaries ooed and awed their way through each color-coded-cluster of prison cells, already populated with prisoners transferred in from various parts of the country. A clear distinction had been made as to who was a prisoner and who wasn't.

Nearly *all* staff were Japanese; imported en masse from Japan, their families included. The doctors wore shimmering white crystalline smocks. The janitors and orderlies wore blue with yellow reflective stripes. The nurses wore an odd green color that could flash brilliant yellow in cases of emergency. The inmates were all relegated to the color of their offense and pod assignments.

Work had moved very quickly on the facility as a whole the moment President De La Croix did what he was told; the only thing he would ever need to do once he got into office, sign the inception documents.

Immediately after the President gave his authorization to create what he thought was a Halfway House-style program, Butch Cairns let his camp know the score and they were flung into action. Across the entire nation, in a flurry of activity, Yoshida Endo's many-facetted conglomerate began inject a caulk made of cash to plug the holes that the Crush had caused. The quick and dirty stopgap measures served to keep the angry citizens at bay while putting up a big enough smoke screen to stealthily construct the new digs for TASC and Endo to begin their testing.

"The world's not running out of oil, no…" Endo's gimcrack campaign of consolation began.

After the last girder was set and the final coat of paint dry, the penitentiary facility came to life, and the prisoner transfer began. All across the country, prison warden's woke to powerfully generous bonuses in their bank accounts. The catch, as the expertly worded letters that accompanied the funds bore out, was that every warden accepting the bonus needed to hand over one to twelve of their most unruly inmates; inmates they simply couldn't stand to have in their penitentiary. Within days the trains arrived, overstuffed with thieves, murderers, and kingpins.

Dr. Yoshida Endo and his right-hand Dr. Kenji Hirasawa had already laid out, installed, and implemented their design. The prisoners arrived and were disinfected prior to intake. Once cleaned and inspected, they were color-coded and taken to their cells by armed guards. After each prisoner was given an orientation packet and after they sat through the short film explaining the intricate feeding process, through which they were to really be receiving their trial pharmaceuticals, they were turned loose and allowed to mingle in the spacious Common Area that connected all of the different wings.

The dignitaries peered over the edges of their respective transports and into the Common Area. The various tunnels leading into and out of the meeting space were decorated with armed guards and a single roving Spyder, all carefully watching every single inmate.

"Excuse me, Mr. Cairns?" Iwao Takamoto, a member of the board of directors, spoke up.

"Yes Mr.... Takamoto-san?" Butch answered with a grin.

"Uh yes, what is to be happening if there is a fight? In the Common Area?"

Before Butch Cairns could answer, a Blue attacked a Red. The immense Blue swing his gigantic forearm and brought it crashing down on an unsuspecting Red's head. The Red's friend turned and began attacking the Blue, but before any real damage could be done, the Spyder dropped square in the middle of the action and from an opening on its crown, rapidly emitted a green plasmatic miasma that disabled all three parties involved. The once-fighting inmates now began to float, unconscious. Amidst the green fog the three inmates remained motionless, suspended in midair. The Spyder extended several tendrils and bound the offending inmates. A port opened in the ceiling of the Common Area and the Spyder disappeared through it, with the inmates, off to return them to their cells.

The crowd of dignitaries applauded the hasty conflict resolution as the transports started up again, ushering them away from their investment.

"Excellent display! Dr. Endo, I would certainly say the board must be pleased with what they just witnessed!" Dr. Kenji Hirasawa bounded with joy after beholding the success of their demonstration. "Sir, I would most certainly wager that the authenticity of that brawl in the Common Area—"

"It really looked authentic? You think so?"

"But of course, sir," Kenji responded. The truth of the Spyder's great expense, leading to the functional existence of only *one* predatory robot, the others being holographic projections, and the fiction behind the 'inmates' brawl' were crucial to the program's success. Endo felt the dignitaries and board members needed a final wow-factor to keep them out of his hair for the duration of the project. "It was meant to look authentic," Kenji continued. "And had I not programmed those inmate simulacra and our lone real Spyder myself, I would've believed it to be real as well!" Kenji continued his sniveling. Growing up without a real father, Kenji had placed Dr. Endo on that pedestal in his mind. Endo, however, was completely unawares as to his elevated status in the mind of his most obsequient student.

The faux fracas had also served as a test of TASC's amplified reality. So far, the inmates were only ones studied under the effects of a False World Projection. The investors and dignitaries were completely unaware that once they were inside the black metal webbing, they were literally in the world Endo had created.

"How do things look for our big roll out?" Endo was of course referring to the implementation of his final piece, the central and true guiding purpose of this facility: the introduction and trial of radically new and untested pharmaceuticals.

"Everything is on track doctor. Tomorrow we begin the introduction of the 'Minerals' the inmates have been told they'll be taking."

"Excellent. Remind me, what is included in the first round?" Endo tested Kenji, as he did with all his subordinates.

"Let's see, for the Reds: dimethyloxycydozine, for the Greens: isopropilenzelaphamine, for the Blues: pyloric ecenalophosphate, for the Oranges, oh boy: Trioxyleniphoracore," Endo whistled when he heard that. "I know," Kenji said from behind a curled and churlish smile. He blinked and cleared his throat. "And for the Yellows: Boronopolyfiazote."

"Ingestion will be at 0900, monitoring will continue 'round the clock, and any anomalies can be disposed of from the Console. If there's anything else..." Kenji trailed off as Dr. Endo's attention had become focused elsewhere.

Dr. Yoshida Endo liked blonde women. Part of his agreeing to uproot his staff and entire body of work for the sake of relocation here to **[LOCATION REDACTED]** required several 'perks' to be guaranteed and readily provided. Blonde women literally at the push of a button was one of them. Endo was fixated on the soft pink button that gently glowed on Endo's personal control console.

During Kenji's rundown of the upcoming big day, Endo had grown tired of Kenji's endless droning and decided to test out one of his perks. Kenji sensed this, and hated feeling second to anything in Endo's eyes. Glaring from behind his tablet, Kenji seethed as he imagined his adoptive father losing his mind amongst a sea of yellow hair.

Endo put Kenji in the back of his mind and continued to scroll through the list of golden-haired courtesans the United States Federal Government was to supply.

"Doctor... Doctor I..."

Endo depressed the button and a giggle emanated from a hidden speaker.

"Yeah, yeah, ok. Whatever you need Kenji, see you tomorrow..." Endo said, turning around in his chair and casually waving off Kenji like he was some commoner, and not the loyal, worshipful, assistant that he was. Endo pressed the button again, and two women entered the room. He did it again, and another beautiful female human strolled in with an air of casual erotica. Endo tittered and continued to press the button several more times. Kenji let out a soft sigh of defeat and exited the now-cramped room, filing out in between the incoming blondes.

Just where do they come from? Kenji silently wondered.

The pneumatic door wooshed shut behind him. Kenji exited Endo's suite in the Tower Keep and depressed the cloth button in his collar used to summon a transport. Within seconds a single-seat, single-wheeled, pod arrived. Kenji had the device scan the chip in his wrist, identifying himself and his residence to itself. In cheery Japanese, the device played a little music and reassured Kenji, having detected the low levels of serotonin. The jovial carrier put-putted with him into the setting sun, eventually arriving at Kenji's modest English-style manor in the Assistant's Row neighborhood of Staff Dormitories.

6 Months Before Unity

DISTRICT OF COLUMBIA

Fresh off of his stunning re-election, Dixiecrat Pickford-Saxby De La Croix sauntered effortlessly down Pennsylvania Avenue. His glorious red beard, Norse-braided and interwoven with golden thread, reflected on the outside what he felt within. Turning from side to side, smiling his radiant golden teeth (he had them polished just for today), he waved to the faithful Dixie's that defeated Ambrose Tarver and those vile and ressurgent Ichabod Whigs. The crowd erupted with joy at seeing their new leader gleam.

Reaching the platform, the suit President-elect De La Croix was wearing changed from a subdued Dartmouth green, his campaign colours, to a pulsing gold and India-Harlequin. Waving and smiling as he ascended the steps, a familiar face caught his eye. The face was that of an iron; hard, flat, rectangular in shape. The slits that passed for eye sockets perked up and the lipless mouth eased into a grin not unlike that of an IRS hybrid eagle-man ready to descend on a tax cheat. The face belonged to Pickford-Saxby De La Croix's childhood friend from the 53rd state, the Greater Bay Area, Mansfield 'Butch' Cairns. The President-elect shook hands with the Vice President-elect in a well-honed fashion they developed as youths. Pickford smiled and mouthed the words 'we did it' before taking the podium.

By the end of his inaugural address, people in the crowd were sobbing, hugging, cheering and jeering. The ocean of humanity parted to allow for the red carpet to roll from the White House to the stage. Pickford and his entourage boarded the carpet which then conveyed them to the new digs. Here Pickford and Butch retired to the Carter Solarium and each picked up their own piece of cutting-edge science: hybridized botanicals spliced with powerful narcotics; otherwise known as narcoplants, developed by Dr. Jean-Paul Lynde LeRoy. Butch was an old pro at this new game. His narcoplant of choice was the black-valium-dahlia. He pinned one on his lapel and buried his nose in another.

Pickford felt that as the newly enshrined leader of the Corporation of the United States, he owed it to the people, Dixies mostly, to expand his mind and truly Amplify his thinking ability. The official narcoplant of the De La Croix administration was to be the opiateorchid but too many adherents were missing rallies and events simply because they had passed out. The orchids were replaced with lysergic Rafflesia and the zealots could not have been happier. Pickford unpinned the lysergic Rafflesia Baletei from his lapel and took a long, satisfying drag on it. Within seconds he was surrounded by a symphony of tangible colors, plants that only wished for his comfort and miniature versions of Jimi Hendrix and Jack Nicholson playing golf on Butch's shoulders. The two men reminisced and enjoyed their time as freshly elected politicians. They both knew this period of tranquility wouldn't last.

Pickford-Saxby De La Croix typically elevated out of bed at 0530am every day. As President, one could not afford to sleep a minute past that, as he had been told. The carpet was soft, his mouth foul. Diamond De La Croix, First Lady et al., still lay sleeping. Her day began at 0630. Pickford was met by his handlers who began anointing him with oils and scents prior to his workout.

After sweating through 45 minutes of ape-sparring, Pickford took a hot MI6-style shower, and followed that with a heaving breakfast. He walked into the Carter Solarium for the days briefing. Pickford moved his daily briefing to this locale in order to be closer to the hybridized narcotic-infused flowers. He had forgotten all about The Crush.

"Good morning Mr. President," Candy, his holosec chirped.

"Good morning Candy, what's new today in the land?"

"Well, you have a meeting with David Sproles and Ralston Thames in regards to the continual handling of The Crush, and from there-"

"The Crush? *The Crush!* Where's Butch!?"

"Oh, um, Mr. Cairns is on his way up here as we speak, sir."

"Good, good, good, I will need a private meeting with him prior to my meeting with the others."

"And the world waits for the President…"

"Cute, just tell Butch to meet me in in the Greenhouse, my nerves are shot."

"Yes Mr. President."

Pickford De La Croix rose again from behind his desk in the Solarium and plodded clear across the property over to the Roosevelt Greenhouse. Relaxing into an opiate-orchid, he felt the tension leave his shoulders, as well as the embarrassment of being the President and forgetting the tremendous financial disaster that is The Crush.

Following suit with China, the US began artificially inflating their GDP after the Petrodollar had lost out as the world's trade currency. Soon Make-Work projects swept the country, and magnificent looking structures began appearing in the Nevada, Utah, Arizona and New Mexico deserts, all of them far too expensive for anyone to actually purchase and live in. The constant construction kept citizens working and raw materials being produced. Staging fake openings and blitzing the newsmedia with glamorous ads for these constructs became commonplace. After a nearly two years though, people began to catch on.

One particular August, a group of conspiracy theorists decided to leave the safety of the Ultranet and venture out to one of these sights in the Nevada desert. At first, they were met by armed guards patrolling the artificial city that was to be New Monrovia. After explaining their imagined goal of catching sight of a certain comet, the guards left them on the outskirts. Biding their time, the group walked along the perimeter until they found a suitable entry point.

Once inside the walled city, the real detective work began. The group mounted cameras on their shoulders and live-streamed their discoveries. Entire neighborhoods of empty houses, walls that crumble with a gentle breeze, fake lawns even. Everything was poorly and hurriedly built. Monrovia was to be a 'gem' in the desert, an Oasis populated with Hollywood stars and excellent schools. The truth was that the US economy was nearly full of saccharine funds and migraines were setting in from coast to coast. The exposé posted on the internet made some take to the streets, others simply wanted to keep working.

"Sir, what I'm saying is the Corporation of These United States is broke. Flat broke. We need income and those plebeians outside this compound are without means to provide any tax revenue whatsoever." Treasury Sec Ralston Thames let out an exasperated sigh, flanked by his lily white mutton chops. "What do you propose, sir? What can we possibly do?" The man's deep black skin provided a pleasing contrast to his shock of ivory hair.

There was a tense silence in the conference room. Although no narcoplants were made available as this was official state business, requiring the clearest of minds, Pickford-Saxby and Butch Cairns had conducted their private pre-meeting under different accords. Pickford's ornate red beard rose and fell with his heavy breaths. Scratching his chin and ignoring the effects of the narcoplants he and Butch had ingested, Pickford leaned forward. He began to speak, but a little bird in black and white stripes in a cage hanging from the ceiling in the corner of the room caught his eye. The little toy had not been there for the meeting on the morning prior. Was

Pickford that high? He couldn't be too sure, but now all he could think of were prisoners.

"What were those figures on the correctional systems? Can we squeeze any more from there?"

"Hmm, funny you should ask Pick," Butch Cairns, having waited for this exact moment, grew a smile and folded his hands on top of a manila folder. During the week leading up to this scheduled meeting, Butch Cairns had been dropping hints and leaving little totems around the White House to get prisoners on the President's mind.

"Why's that?"

"Well, I have here a panacea. I have the answer."

Is Butch more stoned than me? The President wondered.

The living phone booth that was Secretary Cairns heaved a deep breath. He next withdrew a pouch from his inner vest pocket. He laid out a sepia tobacco leaf and filled it with the contents of the small pouch. With his baseball-bat fingers he delicately rolled a rustic cigar. He ran the tube under his nose and inhaled the aroma of potential. He then lit the small log and swirled the smoke in his jagged maw.

"Butch, what are you trying to say? Spit it out!"

"Mr. President," Butch Cairns exhaled a tempest. "I'm saying that I may have a solution to the Crush." Smoke continued to float out of his mouth and dance on his eyebrows.

Pickford-Saxby De La Croix sighed, rubbed his tired eyes, thought of his wife and said "Whatever could that be, Butch?"

"Sir, if The Crush counts as a depression then call this the ultimate anti-depressant."

Pickford's right eyebrow peaked

"Yoshida Endo, whom you met at your inaugural ball, has proposed a generous offer that you would be foolish to refuse."

"Watch your mouth, but go on." Pickford was hungry for the idea now.

"Endo has offered the lucrative hand of his pharmaceuticals conglomerate to help the US recover. His idea is genius and will, with time, be palatable to the public."

"With time? Palatable? What the hell are you talking about Butch?"

"Endo wants to fast track his drug testing and get them onto the market sooner, and frankly what better way to test drug interactions than by mass trial and observation? Confined test subjects, controlled environments and round the clock medical care."

"No US citizen will buy that. We're broke and desperate but we're not animals… Not yet."

"That's the best part! He wants to do it on *prisoners*."

The words hit President De La Croix and echoed.

Really, what's wrong with it? He pondered for a few minutes.

He got up and paced around the greenhouse. He summoned his pipe and Amplified tobacco.

"Let's do it."

"Good! Great! I'm glad you agreed. I say that, because we've already started. In fact, the facility is already up and running!"

The other three men in the room, ignored and forgotten by their President and his VEEP, gazed at Butch

Cairns, dumbfounded.

"Hm hm, yes, indeed, we've already begun this little venture. Here, in the heart of the **[LOCATION REDACTED]**." Butch Cairns opened the manila folder and laid a holotab on the coffee table between the striped couches. From it projected a map, showing a blinking dot where the facility had been constructed.

"Remember signing off on a project back when you were just Candidate De La Croix, that we said we would legitimize after winning the White House for the second time, when we could really fuck around?"

"You mean Project Kumo?"

"That's it."

"But, how could you have started that without me being President yet?"

"Well, you're getting into trade secrets, but hell, you *are* the President. Gentlemen I'm going to have to ask you to sign these agreements saying this meeting never happened and that you all were elsewhere during the divulsion of the following information." Cairns produced the documents and the three visiting cabinet members cautiously signed.

"Good. Well Pickford, I paid to have you elected so we, you and I, can heal the country's financial wounds together. I went ahead and assured Endo over at TASC of a Dixiecrat victory and he provided the manpower. Here, look at it." Cairns' nonchalance in casually admitting he had rigged the Presidential election passed with silence.

Butch Cairns now leaned forward and fiddled with the holotab. The holotab proceeded to emit a 3D construct of a large wrought-iron-looking bird's nest with a domed tower rising from the center. Really it looked like a fallen chocolate cake wrapped in layers upon layers of black spider webbing and Christmas lights. Inside the structure were what looked like clusters of grapes all connected by shimmering brass tubing.

"Is this an open-air facility?"

"No, it looks like it but there is an ionic field covering every opening on the outer layer of the webbing. We went ahead with this design as it makes it easier to casually glance around and see if anyone is hiding where they shouldn't."

"This is incredible."

"Wanna go see it, for real?"

"Of course! Candy? Clear my schedule please, I'm going on a bit of a field trip."

"Yes Mr. President."

With that, the meeting was over, and the four men left to board Air Force One and head to the **[LOCATION REDACTED]**.

Warren G. Harding Above-Top-Secret Penitentiary

"Gentlemen, as both your Vice President and newly appointed Secretary of Incarceration, allow me to welcome you to the Warren G. Harding Federal Research Facility and Correctional Institution, tucked away here in the **[LOCATION REDACTED]**."

Mansfield Cairns stretched his arms in presentation of the rushed facility. The Japanese translator geishas informed another group of stockholders and scientists now entering of the current goings on for a tour.

"Lemme guess, you've had *this* all arranged in advance too?"

"Yes sir, Mr. President, the timing was perfect! We got here just after the scientific delegation from the EU."

"The EU?"

"Yes, y'see Mr. President, when in the area of economic recovery, one must keep all potential sources of income viable and fresh, ready to produce when needed. The EU's potential involvement only means *more money*."

The President really was impressed.

"Well Butch, you've certainly outdone yourself. I approved the new title you anointed yourself with back there with the knowledge and trust that this will not get out of hand. Tell me again, is my trust misplaced?"

"No sir, together we will pull this country from the bowels of poverty and we will make billions in the process."

"That's what I needed to hear."

The two men joined their departing tour group, Fidel Castro XL cigars hanging from their lips.

The facility was vast and colorful with a labyrinthine, almost Edwardian, air to it. TASC moved into the facility with a frightening swiftness. Within days the intricate staff dorms had all been constructed and populated. The buildings themselves were a sparkling opalescent white with orange and lime green accents. Obtuse foliage almost overran the dorm and lab areas.

After observing the grounds, the dorms and the recreation facilities, the group was taken via driverless people-mover to the Lord Warden's manor.

At the top of a hill, overlooking the entirety of Onogoroshima Island, was an exact duplicate of the Carson Mansion found in Eureka, California. Around the house were well maintained terraced Japanese bonsai gardens. The walkways were lined with tea bushes, and there were stone lanterns and torii gates laid out in a proportional manner; the entire scene was beyond soothing to the eye. The Lord Warden chose to occupy his free-time with such pursuits, as the steady consistency of maintaining delicate, intricate, life helped balance out the intensity of classified pharmaceutical prison oversight.

The trams filled the roundabout at the base of the pathway leading to the front door. Here the guests were greeted by the Lord Warden himself, Samuel Taft. Wearing a kimono, the large black man also wore gold pince-nez glasses. His massive hands clasped together, Samuel Taft casually welcomed the group.

"Hello everyone. My name is Samuel Taft and I have been appointed as Lord Warden over this facility. Previously, I served as overseer at Leavenworth, Victorville, and Florence ADX. I have taken the liberty of learning Japanese in order to create a more transparent work environment. I live here, in the big house, with my wife Allison. In fact, here she comes now." Lord Warden Samuel Taft went on to repeat the exact same statement in smooth and impressive Tokyo-chic Japanese.

The group of suited and kilted men reacted to the bilingual oration with a pleased awe. They next turned to observe the elegant Mrs. Taft descend the stairs that led to the main garden walk.

"Hello, konnichiwa." Her voice was silk in the ears of all men present. Her kimono matched Samuel's and her deep black hair was accented with gold strands, much like the great red beard of President De La Croix'.

"Well gentlemen, I have work to return to, but I must admit that am very much looking forward to this evening's banquet. Welcome to Warren G. Harding." Again, the same statement was reiterated in perfect Japanese. Lord Warden Samuel Taft then smiled, his white teeth accented by his deep black skin, and led Mrs. Taft back up the stairs and back to the big house.

"So Butch, will we actually get to see any of the inmates?"

"You mean patients, sir."

"Patients? I guess so. I want to see inside there." Pickford-Saxby De La Croix pointed at the imposing structure. "I want to see exactly how the process works."

"Well Mr. President, you're in luck. We have

another short film after luncheon to explain how things go around here. You'll like it, the same actress you fawned over in intro video is the host in this little snippet as well."

"Gaia Pany again?! Ooo in that case..." President De La Croix reached into his plaid coat pocket and retrieved his cigar case. Clicking it open, he inhaled deep. The woody smell served as his personal reward for making good decisions. He carefully chose a green Vega, his third cigar of the day already, and lit it, letting the smoke take his worries away.

Stanton Finch woke up with the rest of the unwashed. They shuffled from their pods, down the black and gold, ornate Edwardian spiral stairs. After the shower, it was breakfast time. Each inmate had their scapula scanned, enabling the delivery of personalized daily vitamins, each in a small metal cup. The pills were swallowed, washed down with pink, sweet smelling water, and the cups returned under the thick safety glass.

Stanton Finch was originally sentenced to death for channeling Ned Kelly in a bizarre incident held outside the Republican National Convention in Boise. Stanton had raised a small army of defectors who were unsatisfied with the government's handling of the Balzac Accord. Stanton and his men donned thick metal armor and stormed the convention claiming loyalty to the British Crown while citing a typo in the Declaration of Independence. The army charged in through the cacophony and killed several lobbyists before being put down by the Secret Service. Stanton had hung back to 'observe' and command his troops, but he was eventually found out and charged.

Stanton's comfort came from his books. He was allowed seventeen books on British and colonial history, which he pored over daily until he had them memorized. His delusions of the Crown taking back what was lost in 1776 became stronger with the dosing that the Flea Circus Program provided, but the doctors saw this and kept it in check. In fact, all the doctors on staff were given exhaustive dossiers on their patients. The doctors were also quizzed weekly on their patients and part of their pay would fluctuate based on successful drug-to-patient matches. For his general good behavior and relative harmlessness in a traditional prison setting, Stanton was chosen to be part of the Flea Circus. The prison he came from had already sent over an allotment of undesirables, but Stanton had a way of being noticed by prisoner administrators when he wanted to. He heard on the grapevine about the others who had already been transferred and drew the necessary attention to himself to garner a transfer as well. Today would mark week one of his involvement.

When the collected mass of incarceration sat down to breakfast, the guard pressed play on the taped news, which was usually 1-2 days old, all the commercials and any references to anything considered "inducing" edited out.

Kenji Hirasawa was the right hand of Dr. Endo. He grew up in western Japan and was part of the delegation that pioneered the genetic re-imaging of Chinese miners to make them more resistant to the microscopic irritants in the mines, in addition to making them far more resistant to explosions and oxygen deprivation.

He was made the right hand in order to oversee the overall quality of the inmates DNA. Dr. Endo trusted him implicitly. Kenji's work was lean and aggressive; cutthroat.

"No. Absolutely not." Dr. Endo shook his head and forced the udon in his mouth down his throat.

"Dr. Endo. This has been my dream. This is why I went to school to splice and dice in the first place. We've come *this far*. Why stop now?" Kenji never broke eye contact.

Dr. Endo leaned back in his chair, chewed what was in his mouth, and took a sip of his Pernod. His watch gently vibrated, indicating an appointment reminder. The doctor's dry cleaning was ready in the Sanitation Ward. "Kenji, I… I can't allow for this to proceed. The Lord Warden and Cairns, oh god Cairns, have their hands in every aspect of this operation. If they hear or see any of your work, they wont just fire you. They'll *kill* you."

"Diplomatic Imm-"

"Nope," Dr. Yoshida Endo cut off Kenji with a sharp wave of his hand. "Didn't you read your NDA? By signing it you and I have given them permission to kill us if we diverge from the original plan in *any way*." Endo thought for a split second of his wife, their mutual mistress, and his cat. Akira the cat, his little feet looked *exactly* like tabi socks, forked toes and all, was by far Yoshida Endo's favorite of the three. The tea in his porcelain cup slowly drew a memory from the pit of his hippocampus in which he was back in Kyoto, picnicking on the former Imperial Palace grounds with his gorgeous Namiko performing the tea ceremony for the first time in front of him. Akira the cat was sitting up purring at his side, respectfully observing Namiko execute the ancient rite with her unique elegance. There was bamboo and fireflies.

Kenji quietly, resignedly, picked at his bee-bim-bop, no longer with appetite. He stood, bowed, and glided out of the white, orange, and green cafetorium and into a driverless transport. He rode through the wrought-iron black thatched web that made the body of the prison and over to his office just above the green psychoactive section of the misshapen cubic spheroid. Kenji reached into his drawer and pulled out his graduation present. The 30-year old bottle of the Yamizaki filled his nose with orange citrus and the luscious bronze flow eased the lines in his young forehead. From his office-pod he observed the nest. He slowly took in all those whose turn it was to eat in the cafetorium. Other doctors and guards flew by on their own driverless transports, like sea life flitting about a reef. The vicious looking Spyder showed its dominance of the prison webs, shining its lights here and there, swinging from section to section.

Yamizaki.

The Tower was beautiful in the moonlight. The Cyclops Keep on top was a psilocybin mushroom rising out of the rot that made the cafetorium.

Reflection.

Yamizaki.

Psilocybin.

The Lord Warden's house… *Oh, what a house!*

Edwardian England.

Feudal Japan.

Yamizaki.

Terraced grounds.

The Lord Warden.

Yamizaki.

That wife!

Reflection.

Dark skin.

Yamizaki.

Ebony breasts.

Psilocybin.

Yamizaki.

Rage.

Viktor Tandy sauntered over to the pharmacy to chat it up with his friend Elias Cobb. Elias was Maori and assigned to the spec-ops unit tasked with guarding the pharmacy.

"Eli! How's digs around here?" Victor's smile was freshly mopped linoleum on an April afternoon.

They shook hands.

"Vik, my buddy, things are great, I mean, they could be if we could ever leave this place."

"Hey it's not *that* bad, we got plenty of R 'n' R… Say, have you gone out for the Mass Rules baseball squad, or have ya gone soft and chose the 'traditional' baseball schema?" He laughed and hit him on the shoulder. "I'm just razzin' ya, I would kill to go, ya know, stretch my legs on the outside a bit…"

"Wouldn't we all…" Elias trailed off and watched the techs fill a few orders. "Meh, at least the pay's good and all this Japanese eye candy isn't so bad *konnichiwa*," Elias smoothly slid at a passing nurse, clearly uninterested.

"Hey buddy, lemme ask you something," Elias recovered from the nurses indifference.

"Shoot!"

"It's these new pills I've seen them pushing out of there," he gestured towards the pharmatic pickup line. "They're these green and blue jobs, never seen anything like it. The prisoners have all gotten really quiet lately and it's making me nervous."

"Who's the ordering doctor?"

"Aw hell, y'know one of them, Endo, Soda, Kurobota, one of them. I don't know. All the forms and things are in Japanese and I missed more than a few days of the language Boot Camp. Something's just not right about it," Elias then produced, and began to chew on a toothpick. His black hair was perfectly cropped and combed over. His facial tattoos rolled like waves on the sea with each nibble of the tiny wooden stick.

"Hey y'know," Tandy replied. "I heard some pretty angry Japanese floating by near the psionic ward a few nights ago, but, really, you hear that everyday, so I don't know if it's related or not, but, I trust these guys. I mean look around you," His arms opened wide to convey the immensity and intricate nature of all that they were surrounded by. "This place is a technological triumph, a monument to human achievement. An entirely self-sustaining holding facility with every need of its employees met and exceeded. I'm raising chickens and pigs, *pigs!* I help out in the orchards on weekends, I umpire 'Trad' baseball games and I'm the new DH for the Denver Dishwashers in the Mass Rules league we have here. My family's happy, I'm happy, c'mon Eli, stop paying attention to what the little men in lab coats are doing and go pick up a hobby in the Hall of Extracurricular Activities! Hey, perfect your Japanese and perhaps *even you* can convince that pneumatic little nurse over there to put on her geisha act for ya, eh?" Viktor winked and clicked his mouth twice, his eyebrows bouncing like an epileptic walrus.

"Alright alright, lay off me. I'll stop by the Hobby

Hall tonight and see what they have. It's just this hunch, this feeling that wont go away. You know I was a beat cop before this and, just as I made detective, I was pulled here. By you. *I know when the milk is about to go bad* and man, things are starting to curdle around here, I promise." Elias nodded with deft confidence.

"Look Eli, I'll have a chat with a doc I made nice with and then I'll come and spoon feed you some relief, how's that?"

"Hey, c'mere a sec," Elias drew Viktor in close to his detailed face. "You know, there's a pile of sharp rocks over by the doctors' dorms… They're all slick and shiny. Hell, I'd wager they're some rare earth ores in those stones. How's about you go ahead and climb out of one of the windows over there, and jump head first onto it, huh?"

"After you princess!" The two men laughed and shook hands again. Viktor strode away to a nearby driverless transport and zipped over to the psionic ward to see the doctor he had made nice with.

"Well Mr. President, did you like the video?" Vice President and Secretary of Incarceration Mansfield 'Butch' Cairns asked through a haze of hookah smoke.

"Like it? Hell, I loved it!" Pickford took a stunted draw on his hookah pipe and coughed for several seconds. "So…" another round of coughs. "Is that it? Is that all that's going on here?"

"Yessir it is, unless of course you wish to see any of the operations already in progress?"

"Naw, I gave it a think during the vidya and inmates make me nervous. Just tell Warden Taft and the others they're doin' their country a great service etc., and get me the *hell* back to DC! I'm-a ss-startin' to get the shhhh-sshhhakes…"

Which was no surprise.

It was well-known, amongst those who needed to, that Pickford-Saxby De La Croix was also addicted to packing tape adhesive. When he needed a fix, an odd drawl would come over his voice and he would begin to gently tremble. He got hooked on the stuff during his time as a teenaged delivery pilot. The adhesive was derived from a tree whose sap was in the nightshade family.

"Your *things* are in the back bedroom of Air Force One, Mr. President."

On the large bed in the Presidential Suite was a case of clear cello-tape and a lighter.

"Sir, I've received confirmation of POTUS currently boarding Air Force One, Secretary Cairns has given us the green light to begin the implementation of the next phase of Amplified Reality," Renee La Fleur, the Lord Warden's assistant watched the large plane taxi toward the private runway.

In the prison cafetorium, the stone-faced ersatz newscaster droned on about the state fair, an adoption drive coming up this weekend…

"Let's hit 'em," The Lord Warden fanned himself with a gunbai fan given to him by the New Imperial Japanese Secretary of War. He was in full Kabuki makeup, a choice made by his wife, worn in imitation of war paint. The tremendous black man leaned back in his chair, his red kimono spilling onto the floor.

"Right away Lord Warden."

The TASC Amplified Reality Engine was initiated, and the throttle fully engaged.

"Breaking news now," the broadcast cut through the closed-circuit prison television system. "We're just getting in that the first black President of France, Antonin Maria de Villepin has been shot while touring the United States. We have immediate reactions from the rest of the EU, most of which consist of calls to arms…" Those in colored jumpsuits and tracking collars were suddenly eager to hear more from the TV for the first time. "…The latest we're now hearing is that the assassin has been caught and arrested wearing what appears to be the insignia of the

PWP, or the People White and Pure militia, an organization that actively promotes Anglo interests around the country more soon…"

The inmates at Warren G. Harding were abuzz. One could certainly say, *induced* even. What does this mean? War? A race war? Battle lines were silently drawn that day in the cafetorium. The sun sliced through the clouds and made the meticulously placed glass mosaic replica of the Sistine Chapel ceiling erupt with colorful brilliance over the inmates.

Cell: #RB1414SRA 1414 Sri Rajneesh Alley

Inmate: FINCH, Stanton

Prescriptions: Levantizine, Methaquanax, Torquizine

Notes: Patient is docile overall. Patient enjoys sewing, shows virtually no side-effects.

Inmate Stanton Finch sat back on his bit of bench real-estate and remembered how sweet it was participating in the British reconquering of the Maghreb. Several years ago, Stanton had defected from the corporation of the United States and served in King Edward IX's Navy under an assumed identity. He was found out, arrested, court martialed, and deported after being caught trying to dig into the ruins of the library of Alexandria. On an instinctual level, he knew how to command and lead men fighting for essentially nothing. War with Europe because of a dead president? Stanton Finch prayed for nuclear Armageddon.

Cell: #BB1123RHW 1123 Robin Hood Way

Inmate: CAVENDISH, Desmond

Prescriptions: Naltrexone, Covert Sensitization, Aversion Program

Notes: Patient responds well to therapy sessions. Aversion and Sensitization courses led by Dr. Svelton are producing desired effects.

Inmate Desmond Cavendish saw the news as a portent. Desmond grew up in Santa Fe, New Mexico. He spent a significant amount of time with his father hunting down the answers to conspiracies. His family even had a second home outside Roswell. From there, it was only natural for him to get into sport scripting. Desmond wrote Super Bowl CXLI, the 2110 NBA Finals (including the crucial missed free-throw), and the 2113 NHL Stanley Cup games 1, 3, and 4. In addition, he composed several NBA Super Teams and drafted numerous decisive trades and even a team relocation. Because of this, his first question was: Who wrote up the assassination? The subsequent thoughts and inner analysis all gathered around the idea of there being a race war in America, and what that meant for his family outside. He decided to ask his wife when she came for her visit on Saturday.

Cell: #YB1901LCA 1901 Langley Collyer Avenue

Inmate: MAZANAS, Alberto (Tito)

Prescriptions: Clozapine, Alprazolam, Levantizine

Notes: Patient is taking on animalistic tendencies that they did not demonstrate upon intake. Patient can be aloof, listless, or hyper-aggressive; stimuli and triggers remain unknown. No longer responds to Dr. Svelton.

Inmate Tito Manzanas had grown a decent amount of body hair since his arrival and initial dosing. The doctors were now chiefly concerned about a correlation. He didn't seem to care too much about the news. Then again, he could also no longer recall the details surrounding his arrest. Nor how he got to Warren G. Harding. His primary concern was quickly becoming whether or not he is being perceived as the alpha of this pack he now found himself in. The other Latin inmates that cloistered around him certainly weren't aware of their stations in said pack, but they didn't really have a choice when it came down to it, did they?

On the specified Saturday, Desmond's Scandinavian wife Elka Albrecktsson arrived on time, at 1315pm. Her blonde curls bounced, her green eyes shimmered, and her curves sat comfortably in a grey pencil skirt and white blouse. Her golden pumps click-clacked down the hallway to the visitor's area. The air she left behind smelled of night-blooming jasmine.

She sat across from him now in the visitor's area, separated by the customary plexiglass. He picked up the receiver.

"Hi baby."

"Hi."

Silence.

"So, you've heard then?" She asked.

"Yeah, they played the news for us today. I'm not really sure how to feel about everything as of yet. Did they say why he did it?" Desmond couldn't help but to look her with doe eyes.

"You mean other than because the French President was Black?" Elka said. "Yes. They've been saying now that the shooter belongs to some racist group and that they were the ones behind the bombings and hate campaigns we've been seeing."

The 'news', provided by TASC to the inmate-patients, had rebranded and repackaged the Cult of Darwin's very real exploits on the outside as a 'Campaign of Hatred' started by a fictional group called the PWP. In order to reduce the chances of an inmate being 'induced' by the broadcast, the information was always presented in passing, in an innocuous and boring light.

Desmond looked down at his Black skin, then back up at his white wife. "Baby… I… I love you." He put his hand on the glass.

"I love you too, Desmond." She put her hand up and matched his. They stared at each other, speaking silently. This was the first time he spoke those words in two years. He was resentful about getting himself sent to prison so he punished himself harder by rendering himself unworthy of her love and attention. The self-imposed exile had now been lifted by the death of the French President on American soil.

The couple exchanged several more words of encouragement for the other, and after another shared period of silent admiration, she tearfully excused herself to go home.

As soon as she was out of the visitor's area, Elka Albrecktsson peeled off her face.

"Fine, fine work Dr. Svelton."

"Thanks! I'd spent the past few weeks studying her every idiosyncrasy. She is a *very particular* woman. Wasn't easy," Dr. Moira Svelton briskly shook her head.

"Well, that's why we brought you in. We knew you could handle it, especially with the in-roads you've made as his shrink… He bought it though, right?" the Lord Warden didn't see the whole conversation, just the last few seconds.

"Absolutely. The fact that he told her he loves her is huge. In session he always mentions how unforgiving he's been on himself for getting sent here. He really feels like he let her down. But he and the others are set. They genuinely believe a race war was just started. Some of them even view the French President as a modern-day Franz Ferdinand." The Lord Warden liked what he heard. "But I must know, why a war? And of all things, a *race* war?"

"Please keep in mind that this is all the doings of secretary Cairns," The Lord Warden responded. "The very same Butch Cairns who happens to own controlling shares in more than a few of our purveyors. The idea behind creating a fake war is that people will allow for just about anything to be done to them during wartime. Food costs more, gas costs more, the government intrudes more, it's basically anything goes when a war's on. Studies have shown that citizens, at times, are even *willing* to surrender their rights just to *feel* safer." He stroked his handle-bar moustache and muttered something to himself in Japanese. "So, with the inmates thinking there's a war on, we can ease them into more, let's say, controllable situations. In addition, the inmates will self-segregate. It thus keeps them from talking to each other about their 'morning vitamins' and the resultant side-effects. Have you seen Manzanas? Inmate number 477955? He's starting to look like he belongs in a zoo! I don't want *anyone* in those pods thinking about what's really going on. Hell, I don't want anyone in those pods *thinking*. Period. "

Viktor Tandy was making his rounds in the north-western Green Block. This ward had been specially designed to house criminals who arrived showing a heavy predisposition for telekinetics. These psionic inmates were already showing more bizarre side-effects from the experimental pharmaceuticals.

Cell: #GB0743MP 743 Mesmer Place

Inmate: MARS, Atherton

Prescriptions: Gabapentin, Anisomycin, Levantizine

Notes: Patient exhibits strong psionic abilities. Patient responds well to Anisomycin. No noticeable reactions to Levantizine.

The already infamous patient/inmate Atherton Mars currently resided in Green Block at the address 743 Mesmer Place. Atherton's crime was killing three people at his local laundromat after getting into an argument regarding Oliver Cromwell, Richard Duke of York, and who made the better Lord Protector. In the heat of the debate, the tall, stringy haired, brown man with sharp cheek bones next saw a white flash while experiencing the enormous sound of an entire cathedral's worth of glass shattering. When he next woke, the taste of rust and dirty formica lined his mouth. The over-starched cloth of the straight jacket irritated his elbows.

It wouldn't be until the trial that he would see the security cam footage and witness for himself the flaming purple halo emanate from his skull. This cerebral emission caused the three others in the room to drop to the ground, convulsing wildly. Shortly after, Atherton would be christened the world's first psionic mass murderer.

Viktor Tandy was a tall box made complete with a perfect chiseled chin and firmly set grey/blue eyes. His toe-headed curls sat tightly on his head. The bullets that are his teeth shone with opalescence in every smile. He smoked Amplified tobacco out of a TASC sanctioned tobacco inhalation device. He stared through the two-way glass at Atherton Mars.

"Free…" Viktor said out loud.

Viktor felt trapped in his work, despite loving it. Every day he would get up, feed his miniature elephant, take a hot salt-shower, and ride the Harding People-Mover from his dorm (more of an apartment really) to the Tower in the center of the complex. Being the Senior Guard, he could float freely from pod-cluster to pod-cluster. In doing so, Tandy had come to see what Amplified Reality did to each prisoner. He noticed some behaving more so like animals than prior to Amplification. He heard rumors of inmates having bad reactions to the meds and being taken to the sick bay, only to return excessively more docile and taciturn. Before the Lord Warden and TASC decided to wag the dog with the whole assassinated-President-of-France-inspired 'race war' going on outside the walls, the inmates were starting to chit-chat and talk of whether or not the vitamins they were now being given were really vitamins at all.

Viktor never considered the moral implications of what was happening at Warren G. Harding. Being a State-Sponsored-Atheist, Viktor Tandy felt he didn't have to. Viktor could never agree fully with the ethics and moral systems laid out by mosques, churches, gurus, business moguls, and social scientists. He willingly chose to set his own moral compass, and the things transpiring around him were all just "part of the job, no ethical or moral inquest needed."

Just prior to the election of Pickford De La Croix, the Samantha Crelm Administration moved to abolish formal religion, and announced the open and credible worship of "what we've actually been worshiping since our nation's inception," i.e. money. Viktor Tandy shouted "hallelujah" during the press conference and emptied his wallet on the table. He danced and whooped around his new deity, embracing his newfound freedom. He then ripped the crucifix from his wall and hurled it into the street. When he did, he noticed others throwing out things like menorahs and prayer rugs, noting that everyone who did so had the same immeasurable expression of joy plastered on their faces. This scene was recreated throughout many thousands of homes, offices, apartments, and warehouses around the country. Nearly everyone who heard the press conference readily embraced Financialism, America's new number one anti-religion.

The only true morsel of classical morality contained within Financialism was a bastardization of the Golden Rule, now known as the more affluent-sounding Platinum Principle: if you don't want it to eventually happen to you, don't do it to them. Across the country millions of people cast out their statues, totems, idols, icons, evil eyes, Taoist mirrors, prayer flags, rosaries, relics, shrines, runes, and artifacts in exchange for 0.01% APR on all loans.

With this new open spiritualization of currency as his new and only moral compass, Viktor Tandy rationalized that he was merely a man doing his job. He did not put these inmates here. He did not covertly work experimental drugs into their diets, nor did he track their results and call it Haute Science. All he did was remain loyally vigilant to any and all security needs asked of him and his department. The Platinum Principle had no real sway in Viktor Tandy's unique case.

Fixed firmly to the outer rim of his ear, the emergency notifier now began to buzz and hum.

"Yes, Lord Warden?" The device was a direct line to the Lord Warden in case *he* needed something immediately. All the department heads wore such devices.

"Hello Tandy, I need you to drop by my office as soon as you can, I have a few things I need to go over with you." The Lord Warden's smooth and laconic voice slithered out of the earpiece.

"Yes sir, be there shortly."

5 Months Before Unity

Presently, Stanton Finch found himself entranced with a kawaii-style pink satin princess dress he had been sewing for about forty-five minutes now. The ruffles were always the hardest part for him to get just right. The spot in his brain that was responsible for the psionic outbursts that landed him in jail began to tingle. Things in the room began to surreally melt and blend together. Stanton shook his head and tried to focus on the dress.

"Fnugging lace..." he muttered.

All at once he saw the reason behind the odd feeling in the middle of his brain. Inmate Atherton Mars, the powerfully foreboding defacto leader of the Greens, due to immense size alone, had entered the sewing pool.

"Why hello there, Stanton." The towering tattooed Indian said with a velvet smoothness in his voice.

"Atherton." Stanton regarded the man but didn't care to take the relationship beyond a vague understanding that they both hated each other.

The problem that Stanton had with Atherton was that Atherton *enjoyed* not being able to control his psionic abilities. From what Stanton could gather, the loose-cannon-like abilities were more than deadly, and that's what kept the weak and easily-bullied cowering in his wake. An entourage of lackeys had accumulated over the past several months.

Everyone in the Green portion of the facility were given psionic suppressants as part of their 'Vitamin regimen,' but Atherton's ability still maintained trace amounts of activity; the exact level of which no one was really sure of, least of which Stanton Finch.

"You've seen the news?" Atherton scanned the room while waiting for a guaranteed response.

"Yes."

"Then you know what's coming." Atherton flexed his powerful brown muscles through his green coveralls and leaned into Stanton, looking him straight in the eye. "Better get ready, white boy." With a wink and couple of patronizing mouth clicks Atherton and his troupe continued their prowling.

Across the facility, every inmate was trying to work out how the race war unfolding outside would play on the inside. Inmates were circulating planted reports from their "outside contacts," designed to segregate the population. Stories of rogue neighborhood watches and families coming under fire were all the rage. The attitudes of the inmates had shifted from a lackadaisical, moribund, group of convicts, to a lively and polarized mish-mashed representation of society as they were being guided to perceive it.

With all this new fervor happening inside and "outside" of the walls, none of the inmates noticed that their meds had changed. None had noticed their doses were not only larger, but more diverse. No one spoke up when the water in the showers began to taste sweet and give off a pinkish hue.

The trick had worked. Endo and his TASC force

now had free reign over the inmate's entire reality. Anything TASC crafted was immediately swallowed and accepted by those who couldn't refuse. No questions, no worry, no resistance. War meant everyone gave up something, and the more intense the reports from outside were, the more readily the inmates were ready to obey.

Stanton himself had just received a handwritten letter from his 'trustworthy cousin' that the Klan had been setting up roadblocks and checkpoints across Georgia to comply with some group calling themselves the People White and Pure brigade which had actually managed to quietly secede a portion of South Carolina. This slice of rogue America had also been successfully defended against Federal troops as well.

Reflecting on that letter as he sat dutifully at his sewing machine, Stanton resumed the difficult lace work he had stopped upon Atherton's arrival

4 Months Before Unity

DISTRICT OF COLUMBIA

President De La Croix walked through the White House hallway, past the camellia room and through the Clinton additions. He noticed the sun pouring through the glass ceiling in the Roosevelt greenhouse. His Prime Minister (the new name for President of the Senate after some deft readjusting of the constitution by VP Butch Cairns and the DixieCrat-controlled Congress), the cloned Teddy Roosevelt, stood by the door to the Oval Office with his solid platinum teeth glimmering in the diamond-based LED lights.

A cigar cloud stretched out gently from the office. "Bully!" Teddy slapped Cairns on the back. Cairns plastered a prickly smile on his face as he fought the urge to assault Teddy, a bout Butch Cairns simply would not survive. Cairns was keenly aware of Roosevelt's physical superiority, so his barbed grin remained as such. The holo screen showed the various accounts already receiving money from TASC and its bogus subsidiaries. The full-figured women in digi-paint "clothing" giggled and entertained the brooding, ego-obese gentleman rulers.

"Look. At. Those. Figures!" Butch Cairns was also

riding a powerful simulated MDMA wave supplied by drastically modified hydrangea, created by Dr. Endo at TASC. "Pickford, I don't know what to say. First the powerful wing-tip to the ass of the dole system and now the 'proposed emergency mining of the rare metals discovered on the moon' WHERE do you get these ideas?"

Laughter erupted in the pale green office space.

Cairns was referring to the explanations given by President De La Croix to congress and the general public when asked about the sudden influx of real monies. He then went on a tear about Kubrick's Moon Landing as the first successful demonstration of Japanese Amplified Reality being unleashed on an unsuspecting mass of humanity: the generation of people known as the Baby Boomers. World War Two was fought and won for them, from their standpoint, and the longest-living generation of Americans ever refused to let go of Nixon's American Dream, let alone entertain any falsehood therewith.

Pickford-Saxby De La Croix was feeling altruistic, thanks of course to the beautiful Rafflesia Arnoldii creeping throughout the office. Patting Butch Cairns on the shoulder, Pickford then pointed to his desk. A horizontal glass tube in a wooden cradle greeted Butch. Projecting from the top of the glass log were three semi-coiled glass tentacles. Inside the crystal log dwelt what appeared to be a living, electric green mesh, similar to algae. This glowing, swaying chartreuse mass took up about 60% of the glass container it resided in.

"That, Butch, right there, it's a creature that they found piggy backing on one of our satellites that trawled deep space. *Real deep space*, not that Kubrick stuff you were talking about. The satellite landed on an asteroid and a piece of this thing latched on and came back." De La Croix took a deep breath from a Rafflesia that a gorgeous green-haired lady from the British Punjab held out to him. Her eyes were soft fire. She smiled a smile that made Pickford feel more secure and at ease than anything he had ever felt.

"How does it work?" Butch leaned forward.

"Well, the boys in the lab gave me one cell of it after putting it through the gauntlet in hyper-time. Turns out the thing reproduces through mitosis. Also, when contained in an anaerobic environment, alá this sealed aquarium, not only does it thrive, but it also Amplifies human brainwaves. I just pull ole Geneviève over in front of me when I'm all alone and she massages my cortex and lets the ideas stream out of me like the old Niagara Falls, y'know before it was dammed for energy."

"Wow, this just wow." Butch was starting to lose himself in the Rafflesia and the girls when—

"Mr. President, you have a holocall, it's Claudio Benvolio, he says it's urgent." The Holosec waited for orders on the arm of Pickford's chair.

"I'll take it in the Nixon room." Pickford got up and strode to the converted WC that was now the Nixon Room. Jets came out of the wall and spritzed his face with TASC Amplified amphets to wake him up again. "Ready." The painting of Nixon and his dog Checkers frowned harder and flopped down, revealing a holopad on the wall behind it. The image of the leader of the European Alliance appeared before him, in full dimensions.

"Buongiorno Claudio, what can I help you steal today?"

"Hmm, nice-a to see you too-a. Now what is-a this my little birds tell me hmm? Testing-a? Using inmates? Printing the money-a?" his eyebrows danced with that last piece of rhetoric. Claudio knew everything and he wanted in on the Geneva-Convention-violating practices now taking place.

"Well Claudio, I have no idea what it is that you speak of, and I wish you the best as you attend to your nation-bloc's crumbling economy. Ta-ta!"

"No! Please-a! Wait! Y-y-you don't want this going public-a, do you? I have-a here satellite pictures of military convoys-a moving through the free state of **[LOCATION REDACTED]**. Do you think-a that NATO and the new UN might-a be interested in seeing these? How-a about-a the American people, no?" He brandished the holophotos like a gun.

"Hmm, do you at least have a plan?" Pickford was frustrated. All he could think of was that green hair…

"Si. I will-a funnel criminals into your country. There is a prison I visited as a boy, in the 53rd state, the Bay Area. Is it viable?"

Pickford's eyes were buzzing. "You mean, *Alcatraz?* That rotting museum?"

"Si. Signore, this-a will be perfecto. I'll send a team to renovatio the facility and as you are experiencing 'financial recovery' you can say the EA needs the prison space. C'mon Pick-a bambino, look at San Quentin. Capacity of 2500, now holding 8500. This-a, will fly."

"…Don't call me Pick, but… Ok, ok, what about

getting your guys here?"

"Ah Signore, this is bellisima. As you know, the Spaghetti Western has returned and put Italia back on the map. I have a team of professionals ready to stage crimes without ever relinquishing custody! Bravo!"

"Hmm." Pickford thought for 2.3 seconds. Of course to him it was as if he'd had a solid weekend to chew it over. "Claudio, are you busy right now?"

"No Signore, the Madame is out, setting fire to *my* money."

"Haha, Claudio, haha, well then come on over, let's celebrate together."

"Haha, yes, ok. I am-a leaving now."

Just outside Verona, Mrs. Benvolio lit a match.

Warren G. Harding Above-Top-Secret Penitentiary

"Bonsoir, Dr. Hirasawa, which project do you care to further?" His holosecretary, a lithe greenish projection named 'Collette,' took the form of a submissive French maid; it was late, and Kenji was alone in the lab.

"Bonsoir Collette, open WGH9-334T7, password: 'eloquence.'"

"Opening."

An eight by fourteen-foot piece of the floor rose. A thin current of electricity ran across the top for sterilization. More compartments opened and soon Kenji's entire project was laid out before him. He brought up the over-sized 3D models of a few choice inmates' genes and let a tear slide down his cheek onto the sparkling white floor.

"Doctor, you may want to see this."

"Yes, Collette?"

She cleared the table and showed him the results of his now shuttered venture. She was right. He had developed a gene therapy that allowed for the test subject to have their DNA completely reimaged. The next evolutionary step of his work with the Chinese coal miners had been achieved. Kenji could now change *any* aspect of a person's genetic makeup, CRISPR be damned, and turn them into anyone or *anything* they wished. The excitement was so much that he completely forgot about what this could mean for his clandestine test subject, Inmate no. 477955, Tito Manzanas.

For years he had wracked his brain and tried every technique and modifier he could get his hands on. The missing ingredient, in the end, was the addition of a compound very near and dear to Kenji, psilocybin.

While at University in Tokyo, Kenji became friends with an Egyptian-Brit, Percival Potiphar Tisch. Tisch fought tooth and nail to get into Tokyo Ika Daigaku to please his mother. Tisch and Kenji roomed for 2 years until Tisch had a change of heart after his mother passed away. During those two years however, Tisch had shown Kenji the wonders of living a naturally Amplified life. They first played around with nightshade and mesculine, documenting everything about their experiences. Tisch believed these drugs opened parts of your mind and enabled immeasurable cognitive advantages. After two years of hallucinogenic research and an amazing academic showing, Tisch bailed.

Just before Tisch flew back to Britain, he and Kenji went camping in Nishi Tanzawa valley. It was here that Kenji's mind was altered.

"These? These are psilocybin mushrooms Ken. This is the penultimate cognitive dredger." Tisch smiled.

"You mean there's one stronger?"

"Well if you can get your hands on human adrenal glands, be my guest, and as you know, LSD isn't for everyone. This though, in a happy, positive environment, this is perfection." Tisch handed him four large caps, six chewable 500mg Vitamin C supplements and a glass of orange juice. "Vitamin C is supposed to boost the effects, let's do what we went to school for." The two munched and swallowed. The fungus tasted like dusty wet clay; a damp crawlspace. The flavors of the 'shrooms didn't sit well with Kenji, but the effects did. For eight hours the two men frolicked through the valley. Each had their own troupe of animals and made-up people skipping with them, encouraging them on. Plants sang and expressed concern for their well-being. They even came across a talking wooden map. Comfort and cheer ruled that night. The best thing, though, to come from that night was the shuttered experiment that now lay on his workspace, five feet away from him.

"ENDO!" Kenji shouted.

More Yamizaki.

In Japanese he uttered just audibly "私は彼らを癒します..." <<I will heal them…>>

Kenji felt that now was his chance. Now was his time to make his mark on the world and to make sure that the entire population is made aware of what has been going on at Warren G. Harding Above Top Secret Penitentiary.

Desmond Cavendish winced as he pushed himself past his personal best in terms of crunches. This afternoon's session would help keep him distracted from his most recent meeting with his wife. Her eyes were different, and Desmond couldn't fritter out exactly why. The light he fell in love with just wasn't there anymore. This now flagged itself in his mind as something he should bring up to his psych, Dr. Svelton. She always was a good listener. Patient and loyal, Dr. Svelton took in all of Desmond Cavendish's angst and frustration and then created methods for him to overcome that which built itself up into a terrible force within his mind.

Desmond cherry-dropped down from the freshly installed pull-up bar in his Blue pod. All at once the whimsical tone announcing the commencement of the afternoon's Medical Ingestion Period sounded. Desmond grunted and slung on his Blue coveralls. A few minutes later, his pod door wooshed open and a guard with a train of other Blues behind him stood waiting. Desmond dutifully walked out of his cell and fell in line with the other patientmates. Thankfully he had been placed in the middle, folded deep into a group of other Black patientmates. The Whites at the front and the Latinos in the rear all glared from amongst their respective groups and leered at the others. The 'race war' was heating up on the 'outside,' according to the 'news,' and tempers within the walls of Warren G. Harding had begun to reflect the "dominant attitude of those outside". Everyone who had an 'outside contact' said something completely different about their experiences in the 'race war.'

Tito Manzanas had a brother and a nephew that came to visit him each week. In the visiting area, Tito would patiently wait, eyeing the clock and the sky through the brief slits in the walls that passed as windows. Tito was of course unaware that just below the window slits, a curious patientmate would have been quickly made aware of the truth as the window slits merely opened to LCD monitors displaying what the administration felt the sky should look like that day.

Tito's brother and nephew arrived every Wednesday at 1400. They had begun to tell Tito, a Red Inmate, of guerrilla tactics being used by White militias all over the country. According to Tito's brother, the White militias were all merely waiting for someone to take the lead. Now that the PWP had sprung into action, the other race-based militia groups had all come out of hiding and had begun their individual plans for racial cleansing. These reports created an attitude of resentment in Tito. Were the White prisoners in here *feeding* instructions to their militia mates outside these walls? Tito couldn't decide, but his nephew would always close their visits with a phrase or two that only watered whatever his brother had planted.

Tito was but one of many, many patientmates that received information like this. Nearly every inmate had a family of actors assigned to play their familiar outside contacts. Most of the time the actors were the patientmates very own psychiatrists. This was done as the doctors caring for their minds would have greater insight into how to keep them fully immersed in the Amplified reality being supplied by TASC. If a child was needed then a small, unmarked, shop nestled in Maintenance Meadow, the machinist/repairman stronghold of Warren G. Harding, came into play. Here fully controllable simulacra were built. The shop was unmarked and largely off-limits due to the paranoia of the Lord Warden. With the bots so realistic and so easy to pilot, the Lord Warden had firm controls placed on access to the shop. To commission a new bot required a personal visit from the Lord Warden himself.

Dr. Gonzalo Martinez, aka Berto Manzanas, had the child simulacra, Tito's nephew, pre-programmed with certain specific trigger phrases designed to further enforce the Amplified reality of a race war engulfing the country.

The line of Blues trudged forward from outside of Desmond Cavendish's pod and down into the Ingestion Theater.

Desmond obediently waited for his turn at the window. The attractive Japanese nurse, in her equally cute and enticing candy-striped uniform, slid Desmond his metal cup with its four odd shaped pills. "Vitamins." Next was the sweet pink water. Desmond opened his mouth to show the guard his enthusiasm for taking his medicine.

Next was one of Desmond's favorite parts of his time here; a visit with Dr. Svelton.

Desmond was ushered into the psych waiting area. The familiar, large, taupe room lush with plant life and comfortable seating, greeted Desmond. He gazed briefly through yet another of the thousands of LCD windows, unaware that he really stared at a computer generated image.

The door to her office opened and Desmond walked in.

"Hello, doctor, nice to see you." Desmond enjoyed his time here. Dr. Moira Svelton had an impeccable resemblance to his wife. Visiting her was like seeing his heart's peahen once more.

"Hi, Desmond. How have you been?"

Feeling the onset of his 'vitamins,' Desmond corralled the rush of unknown nutrients and continued, "Very good. Elka dropped by last week. She looked..." Dr. Svelton held her breath. "She looked good. Her eyes were dim, something was troubling her..." he trailed off staring at a narcobonsai on the doctor's desk.

"Do you like that, Desmond?" Dr. Svelton took note of the tripomorpizol taking effect. Furiously she wrote on her notepad as she didn't have much time. The effects of this frontal-lobe suppressant didn't last long. "It's a bonsai of a non-addictive opium and passionflower hybrid."

"It's... gorgeous..." Desmond had begun to drool.

"Desmond, I need to know, do you know who you are, or where you are, or who I am?" These questions were crucial indicators of what stage the tripomorpizol was working at.

"I... stole... You... Elka?..." He blathered on.

The last remark worried her. *Had he seen through my disguise?* She thought.

"Disguise?" He said out loud, slightly more lucid.

"I didn't say anything..." she said cautiously. *How could he have heard that?* She thought.

"Heard what?" Desmond, now almost completely

lucid sat upright in his chair across from the blonde, curvaceous doctor.

For a time, neither person spoke, or thought.

Then, just as Dr. Svelton moved to speak, to dismiss the session, Desmond's eyes rolled back in his head and he slumped over in his chair.

Moira leapt over her desk and dove to keep him from falling out of the chair.

"Desmond! Wake up!" she called into his face.

All at once his eyes returned, but did not focus on her, and to her surprise he griped her forearm with tremendous force. She grit her teeth and began working to peel his thick, dark fingers loose.

After she popped the index finger off, her own eyes rolled back and she collapsed into a heap next to Desmond on the floor.

An unknown amount of time passed.

Desmond came back first.

"Doctor... I... I'm so sorry." He began, until he noticed her motionless on the floor. "Doctor?"

She woke with a sharp gasp.

"Desmond? You... you love me?" She said, her eyes suddenly hopeful and empathetic.

"Wha... hold on, wait." Desmond's mind was flooded with information. He saw lecture halls, a graduation party, and eventually himself, sitting across from himself.

Moira Svelton's mind was now awash with fresh information. She saw who she had become in Desmond's eyes. She saw the internal conflict he dealt with in remaining loyal to Elka, despite his feelings for Moira.

Desmond now saw another, vital piece of information with powerful clarity.

"You're... you've been Elka for several *months* now?" The ire was clear in his voice and facial expression.

"Desmond..."

"Why!?" He roared at the woman.

"Desmond this is too much," tears were rolling down her cheeks.

"Where's Elka?"

"Desmond,"

"Tell me! NOW! What happened to my wife!"

Getting to her feet, Dr. Svelton slowly walked behind her desk. After several seconds of furious typing, she brought up a folder full of videos. Beckoning Desmond to her side, she slid a keycard she wore around her neck and the videos began playing.

Desmond watched his beloved Elka, the real Elka, cavorting with himself. Every single frame of every video shown contained footage of him and his wife, heavily enjoying their time together.

"What..."

"Desmond, how much did you see, in here?" she indicated her head.

"Just, just you, dressing up like her..." Desmond was in daze. "I need to sit down."

"Desmond, do you really..."

"Love you? Well, now that I've seen Elka is nowhere near me, and I've been interacting with you this whole time. I mean, how could I not be in love with you. You're the only one here who treats me like a human being…"

Dr. Moira Svelton saw a flash of her cheating husband and cursed the wedding ring in her desk drawer.

"Desmond, I—" Just as she started, Desmond seized up.

Again rushing to his aide, Dr. Svelton performed the standard first-aid necessary for someone having a mild seizure.

After the episode had concluded, Desmond shook his eyes free from their fixed gazed and blinked several times.

"Dr. Svelton? Where am I?"

"Desmond, you're in my office, do you remember the last few minutes?" she asked with desperation in her voice.

"I, I was here. Then..." his head ached more now than ever before in his life.

"If your head hurts then don't try to remember, it's ok." Feeling emboldened by their earlier exchange, Moira planted a tender kiss on Desmond's lips.

Desmond accepted the kiss at first, but then drew back. "I'm sorry doctor. Elka was here last week aaand-wait." Desmond had a glimmer, an inkling.

"I love you too, Desmond." Dr. Svelton had let her defenses completely fall. Whatever these two had shared mentally not two minutes prior to this exchange was so intense, so deep, she had already let him into the deepest parts of herself.

A light began flashing on her desk.

"Shit," she said bitterly. "Our time has drawn to a close, Desmond." Rising to her feet, she forcefully walked over to her desk and withdrew a handkerchief to clear the tears from her face.

"Doctor, I'm not too clear on what happened today in session, but I have this, this feeling inside my brain. I feel like we've connected in a very intimate way."

It was at that moment Dr. Moira Svelton made her decision.

The following day, In the northwestern part of Warren G Harding Federal Penitentiary, Desmond sat up in his Blue pod. His section of the grape vine bore much fruit. The pods were clustered here in a beautiful azure array; electric cyan grapes kept from falling to the earth by the grace of black iron webbing. The guard arrived a little later than normal and slid Desmond his morning 'vitamins.' The man then closed the latch and resumed whistling along his route. Desmond considered his tray and recited his daily regimen for his own amusement. "One green for vitamin A, two yellow for vitamin B-complex, a pink for digestion and–" he stopped. On the tray was a new pill. Large, blue, bespeckled, and banded. It looked more like a marble than a vitamin. The oblate spheroid beckoned him, drew him into its glowing blue belt.

"Eat Me," he swore it said.

"Okay," Desmond opened his mouth, unquestioned and whet, and his stomach accepted the offering. As it rolled past his larynx he felt a tickle. "Oh boy, this is… This is …tHiS iS…" his eyes followed a light into the back of his head and he was out. On his bed, Desmond convulsed and then rose, not to his feet, but to a floating position in mid-air. Of his many amenities for good behavior, his poster featuring the entire cast of The Simpsons was his favorite. He ebbed toward the cherished item and stared. One by one, each of the characters began to hold up letters. The letters now formed words. The words told Desmond to raise an army and take back the prison, take it and use it as a base for other Blues to organize and march on the capital. Desmond laughed himself into twenty minutes of aerial summersaults and took up the commission. He swore a blood oath to the poster and passed out, vital red liquid dripping from the hand he bit to symbolize the deal with his yellow skinned demigods. What Desmond, and the staff at WGH, didn't know was that he was a psionic. He belonged in Green. However, his abilities were long suppressed by the dynamic duo of his parents and their suffocating religious practices. This denial of his natural ability caused numerous episodes similar to the one Desmond shared with Dr. Svelton. The result? A life of crime born from the forced rejection of his own evolution.

Stanton was tired. His mighty beard looked to him like the tail of a sick tiger; it hung, moved around in a rather morose manner, stunk. His once lively Amplified facial hair was now mocking him. Stanton chalked it up to too much time in the pen, stress from the ongoing 'race war', and the constant adjustments made by prison officials. Never once did Stanton think the vitamins all the other prisoners were receiving as well could be the source of his now languid facial apparatus. The books on Olde English history sat on his shelf, lifeless. He'd read all of them four times over, all sixteen of them.

It was 0917am. A guard appeared outside his pod with his vitamins. The little metal cup looked slightly different but Stanton didn't care. He stared at his pills, today there was a new one, a small blue ball, dotted in orange with an electric blue glowing band around it. *Pretty*, he thought, *maybe this will cause the sun to part my clouds.* He swallowed his pills and drank his water. He felt something on his lips and wiped his mouth to reveal a long gray streak on his arm. He smelled it and got a nose full of metal shavings. "The fnug is this..." he said out loud. He licked his lips, they tasted sweet. Lo and behold he was right, he was already starting to feel better. In fact, it seemed, with every breath he took, he got happier, lighter. Stanton hadn't had any Amplified cannabis as an inmate, they only grew that for the guards and gave the non-Amplified stuff to the test subjects; something about the Amplification process messing with the frequencies given off by the meds.

Stanton flopped onto his cot and started giggling. His beard was revivified and going wild now. He noticed a particular plant suddenly growing all over his pod. Slow but sure, an ivy-like plant was crawling out of every seam in his pod and engulfing his room. He laughed and so did the plant. An overwhelming sense of calm and acceptance took him by the eyes and led his head to his bookshelf. Out of a book extolling Winston Churchill's drunken cartography strode, well, Winston Churchill; albeit a cartoon, and really more John Bull than Churchill.

"STANTON!" his little voice grew to over 50 feet tall.

"Hehehe…yesss?" the 's' lingered, he let it, it made his teeth vibrate.

"STANTON! You have been exceptional in your devotion to the crown, have you not?"

"T-t-t-the Crown. I love the crown. I love King Edward IX, the New Raj, yes yes yes yes yes yes…" The plant was dancing to music that wasn't on.

"STANTON! I hereby commission you to oversee the transition of this facility *back* to the crown. This structure and its grounds belong to Mother England do they not?"

"Yes"

"You do yearn to serve The Crown and its interests, do you not?"

"A-a-a-anything f-for the crown!"

"Good. Reclaim this land. Bide your time as you build an army. *Kill all* who oppose."

Stanton burst into an uproar of agreeable laughter

as Winston John Bull Churchill opened the cover to his book and dove in, slamming it shut behind him. Stanton enjoyed the rest of his time writhing and drooling in a world all to himself.

Every morning for the next one hundred days, he and Winston Bull would meet and discuss the plan of attack. He recruited other White inmates, at Winston's behest, and instructed them on what to do and when. Each new recruit coaxed another 'Saint of The Garter' to come out from within the books that lined his cell. There was Disraeli St. George, Elizabeth Palmerston, Henry Nightingale, Neville Lloyd George, and so on.

Every inmate in this facility was and had been taking Levantizine, the new TASC drug, for nearly two months now. This little green pill had an undocumented side effect of making the user complicit with almost anything presented to them after enough of it had been pumped into their system. Thus, not one of the other inmates questioned Stanton, despite his beard's strange behavior.

4 Months Before Unity

San Leandro, California

Marlin Fevers woke up to his favorite morning radio show Woodsy, Marty, and Gravy. Currently Woodsy, the ringleader was ribbing Marty for committing another classic Marty-foul-up.

Laughing as he made his way to his bathroom, Marlin's wife Pepper rolled out of bed and began her daily stretching routine.

After a robust breakfast, Marlin got dressed and headed out on his bike for the BART station. Marlin and Pepper Fevers lived in the thriving downtown area and his bike ride never went longer than seven minutes.

The BART train was on time, something that Marlin was thankful for as his body was on a tight schedule. Each morning, prior to starting his commute, Marlin took a powerful pre-workout hemodilator. The concoction forced his veins to dilate and flooded his body with nutrients. This put Marlin in a hulk-like state of readiness. Typically, the flush, as he called it, hit him in the Transbay Tube. By the time the train arrived, he would charge up the stairs at Montgomery station and prime his body for the early morning, pre-work workout. His entire firm, a rag-tag IT outfit nestled in the heart of downtown

San Francisco, had memberships at the gym two blocks from their HQ.

At his lunch break, Marlin left the office alone. He liked his coworkers, but he didn't care to know of their lives outside of work. He had a great wife and kids and his art kept him more than busy.

Lunch today would come from a newly opened ramen shop on the Embarcadero. The ramen was a thick tonkotsu base with black garlic oil woven in, Marlin's favorite.

As he soaked in his dish, he looked out over the bay and something caught his eye. There was lively activity on Alcatraz. Putting down his chop sticks he tried to focus in on anything of note. Construction crewmen here and there, a few boats. He then noticed that none of the famous tour boats were out on the bay. For years he had come to be as any local was, ignorant of most tourist-related activities within their own locale. But the absence of the familiar yellow boats was indeed worth noting.

Marlin checked the time and saw he had enough to investigate, if only for a short while. He hustled down to the pier and caught the F Muni Train to the Tourist Dock near Pier 39. Marlin noticed the Alcatraz tour companies had all, overnight, gone out of business. Marlin next turned his attention to the island itself and saw the workers on the island were wearing green, white, and orange jumpsuits.

Warren G. Harding Above-Top-Secret Penitentiary

The following morning, in the showers, Stanton bathed next to an inmate that had become a close ally. It was at this juncture that Stanton decided to make this man his precious Leftenant.

Hurston Matchstick Chisholm let the hot water ease the pain in his forehead. Hurston was taking psionic suppressants, which resulted in torturous migraines.

"Hey Hurst, I need to talk to you. *I've received my calling.*"

"Calling? Stanton, what the hell are you talking about, and when did you get an accent?"

"I don't 'ave an accent. This is just 'ow I talk. Listen, you and I know we don't belong locked up in 'ere, in an *illegal* facility built on *illegal* laws backed by an *illegal* government. We stand on the *King's soil*, not that of a 'republic.' Innit?"

"Well, the US has been a corporation since 1928 so, you are right there. Crazy."

"Crazy?!" Stanton's voice rose. "What's crazy is the fact that the White House 'as free reign over the fate of a population that belongs *not* to itself. Look, this war has touched me."

"Has it?"

"Oh yes. My eyes is open now. I'm lookin' 'round,

so keep your eyes and ears open. I know at least a few of the others 'ere are PWP members and I plan on usin' them to lead my charge."

"Really." Hurston was flat-faced and bored.

"Hmm hmm, you may smirk and think me wrong, but thass ok. I want you to. That'll just make my ascent and seizure of this facility that much more legendary. I'm raising an army Hurston. We're going to take this place first, then the White House. I will hand-deliver this wretched country back to its rightful owner, King Edward IX."

"Wow. Well, Stanton, I wish you the best. My head feels like insects are digging around and having a serious discussion on harmonizing world religion. I'm going to get some meds."

With that Hurston Matchstick Chisholm turned off his spigot and left Stanton standing there. Stanton had failed at a major recruitment and began to feel anger grow inside his stomach. As he turned to bang his fists on the tile wall, out of the steam came another man. It was Atherton Mars.

"Stanton."

"Atherton."

The two men stood nude in the steam, keeping their eyes locked on the other. The rumor of Atherton having the ability to kill with his mind had made the rounds, as did a legend of Stanton being fiercely pro-white but anti-American.

"I heard what you said to Chisholm."

"Did you?"

"Oh yeah, and I want in. I had some contact with

the PWP before I got pinched and they're a serious organization. If you're serious about returning this land to the crown and erasing that false seat of governance in that stinking swamp, I'm in."

Stanton eyed the imposing brown man. The rambling yet forceful words of Winston Bull and Disraeli St. George had fortified him against any resistance. He then remembered the Old Raj, the New Raj, Gandhi's fervent desire for both Indian equity alongside Whites, both equally subjugating the Blacks, and moved to accept the help being offered from the Commonwealth. "In that case, let me be the first to welcome you brother. God save the King."

"God save the King."

The two men shook hands and departed from the showers. A few other White inmates overheard the exchange and followed the men to the changing areas where Stanton told them to wait until outside recreation to talk more.

On the cricket pitch, the men Stanton had recruited all gathered and established their organization. The moniker unanimously chosen was The Sons of Stanton. From this point forward any current and future members were to communicate by sock-message. One would carry the communique in his sock, to either another courier or to the intended recipient. Once the two had met up, they would exchange socks and thus the messages. Stanton wanted the army to be raised quickly, but not so quick that they would be found out. The words of Winston Bull echoed his ears "Bide your time in building an army…"

Every day the ersatz news added more fuel to the fire of racial tension in the prison. Kenji's plan was in full swing. The blood-concealer he had crafted was seamlessly hiding the lead, psilocybin and other fun ingredients he had been adding to individual regimens. Stanton Finch accepted his daily psilocybin trips as open-eyed-dreams; glorious visual holy writ given especially to him by the spirit of English patriots.

Weeks began to pass. Each week, Kenji chose a new inmate after going through their dossiers and added a new piece to their puzzle. Some inmates got lead poisoning, baffling the support staff. Others began exhibiting strange new abilities. Atherton Mars was only the first inmate to demonstrate Amplified power in the manner Kenji sought. Felix Teizel, inmate #433390 and also a psi, managed to wrap the plastic paneling in his cell around himself, causing almost immediate suffocation. Alfred Munn, inmate #567234, in for several acts of violence against his former employer, demonstrated a Jekyll/Hyde ability to morph into a hulking, crying, beast when pushed far enough.

The TASC reps received these and other much more gruesome reports daily.

The size and weight of the TASC coffers had grown so large that the board in Nara simply ignored any bad news coming from the facility, instead focusing on the wealth of material success and the plethora of good reports that almost drowned out the bad. Almost. President De La Croix never saw a single negative report; Butch Cairns saw to that.

After several weeks of ersatz war reporting, the agitation in Warren G. Harding Above Top Secret Penitentiary was at a boiling point. Desmond Cavendish's Crows had been expertly dispatching Stanton's men covertly in the showers and on the various fields of recreation. Desmond had suspected something was up with his regimen of pills and had been able to conceal their false consumption. He suspected something strange after several experiences similar to Stanton's; the only difference was Desmond's crushed soul and the bizarre experience in Dr. Svelton's office.

With the sudden drop in medication however, Desmond's disquieting thoughts, thoughts which he used as fuel to build his converse to Stanton, had come to overwhelm him. He slept less, ate less. In the time he cut out his regimen, Desmond had gone from cunning prison gang-leader to a depressed lump. The loss of and misdirection regarding the woman he fought for his entire life was proving to be too much.

The other members of his gang, The Black Leather Crows, were starting to notice Desmond slipping.

"Eh man, you seen Desmond lately?"

"Yeah, he looks down. Real down."

"You think, he gonna *run*?"

"Run? Shit, man, you have a look around this place? This prison is a POWDER KEG! E'ry day there's another fight, usually where I'm tryna eat! Run!? Run where!?" The man was clearly incredulous. "There's a war on outside, there's a war on inside, and on top o' that, my cousin on the outside, yeah, he say there's actual fightin' goin' on now. House-to-house brawls an' all that. Ain't nowhere to run *to!*"

"Yeah… but look at 'im… He been starin' out that window fuh the past fortnight, non-stop."

"Yeah thass true, I 'unno man, he could run, he could hang hisself. Things here have been *weird* to say the least. If I could bet, I'd bet on the good ol' bedsheet-noose!"

"I got two packs of cigs ridin' on him runnin'."

"For real? Who's bookie?"

"Shhhh, you too loud!"

Several others nearby heard the word 'bookie' and started getting antsy.

"Sorry, my bad."

"All good, 's'all good, just keep your voice down. There's a White dude in Red Block on Sri Rajneesh, he's sorta obsessed with England, but, he'll take your bet. Oh, you gotta come with your bet in hand too, no credit."

"Gotcha. Man, I picked up a carton from the commissary that 'fell off the lorrie', eh? I'm in Red Block today, pushin' the book cart. I'll see him then…"

3 Months Before Unity

Warren G. Harding Above-Top-Secret Penitentiary

"Collette?"

"Yes, Hirasawa-san?"

"I need you to prepare the results of Project Swap for me to disseminate to Dr. Endo, please."

"One moment," The holosec, presenting itself as Kenji coded it to, once more as a French maid, closed its eyes and collated the data. "Would you like it made Presentation-Ready?"

"Yes please, merci Collette," Kenji said with a grin.

Once everything was in proper order, Kenji had Collette transfer the entirety of the presentation and its accompanying data to the memory stick built into his right hand. Taking a deep breath and clearing his mind, Kenji left his manor in Assistant's Row and took the communal transport system to the luscious Onogoroshima, otherwise known as Director's Island. Here, Dr. Endo and his seven department heads lived in Amplified luxury. Taking full advantage of the R & D department at TASC labs, Endo and his peers had created a virtual island paradise.

Kenji came in on a catamaran and lodged his

seacraft in the sandbar outside of Endo's villa. He paused to notice the holographic, but startlingly realistic, surroundings. Just as he reached to touch the frond of an enticing, lush palm tree, Endo appeared.

"Hello Kenji, what can I do for you?" Outside of office hours, Yoshida Endo detested work related items. Kenji greatly appreciated this, and very few other things, from Endo. However Kenji was raised in the US before returning to study in Japan, so many of the nuances about Endo confused and put off Kenji from time to time.

"Well, sir, we had some free time and see, I have this project that I have been working on. Well actually I have several, but this one-"

"Kenji, you know about my policy."

"I do sir, I do, but, with that policy rigidly in place, how can we develop and expand upon-"

"Yoshiiiiiiii" the erotic and cat-like calling of Dr. Endo's name began to emanate from the doctor's abode.

"I'll be right there Lana!" The doctor called to the voice from the villa. "Look, Kenji, we'll talk about this tomorrow when our shift begins, ok?"

"But doctor, this is at least the tenth time you-"

"Hirasawa-san! I have spoken!" Endo now threw up his hands and gruffly looked Kenji in the face. Using his surname meant he was being drastically serious now. "Now look," Endo waggled a finger in Kenji's face. "If I open up my out-of-office hours to *you*, then I'm opening them up to everyone. We'll cover it tomorrow. Period." With that Yoshida Endo turned and trudged his way up through the white sand and into his imposing 'oceanside' manor.

Kenji Hirasawa watched in defeat as his boss and tormentor, having dismissed his very own right hand, resumed his debauched off-work activities like it was nothing.

Kenji did have a point. There had been at least ten occasions when Kenji had attempted to show Dr. Endo his own personal body of work. He had been eager to share his recent findings on his Chinese Miner project that began when he returned to Japan for graduate studies for several years now.

Kenji had sliced, diced, and spliced the DNA of hundreds of different men who had "proudly dedicated their lives to China, and the mine," in the words of the Chinese company sponsoring the trials. The men could now breath in sand and not lose a single percentage point on their pulse-oxygen readings. After two years of experimentation, the miners could also endure explosions the equivalent of a standard issue pineapple grenade. The miners own skin would react to the approaching invisible energy waves emitted from an explosion and vibrate at a frequency that cancelled out the concussive force of the blast.

Kenji had a masterful presentation prepared to share this and one more intriguing piece of body of research. Kenji eagerly yearned to share the results of genetic re-imaging when integrated with psilocybin-derived extracts: just like their favorite childhood superhero, a miner with psilocybin interwoven into his genetic material could mold and manipulate the physical objects within their reach. During his experiments, Kenji had noticed a region of the mind surging with activity once the psilocybin had been formatted to integrate with the body, as opposed to being used or absorbed as nutrient processing by the body.

The implications were tremendous. These mindless outcasts of society could be transformed into controllable, useful workers. Workers that could thrive and provide unheard of levels of productivity despite the conditions they were to be working in. This research could revolutionize the emerging prisoner housing crisis and solve the need for cheap labor in one fell swoop. Kenji Hirasawa knew *his* name could potentially be gracing a new grant or wing of a university. Kenji saw *his* name crest the top of a lecture hall back at his Alma Mater in Massachusetts.

On the ride back to Assistant's Row, Kenji kicked around all of this in his mind. He typically would water these thoughts and dreams until at last he left his mental garden of disappointment. This time though, before he put down his watering can, he noticed a new plant in the garden. He had heard of this plant, yet he had never actively sought to grow it. *Ten times*, he thought. With that echoing in the depths of his consciousness, he now made a special area in his mental garden for this new plant to grow. For the first time in his professional career, Kenji now let grow within him *resentment for his superior.* Anger, disgust, and most hurtful of all, envy, now had a place to well up within him. The best food, Kenji felt, for this new attitude came from a bottle; only alcohol would best suit this situation.

No narcoplant existed that provided the same goading, grinding death of judgmental ability that alcohol did. Narcoplants were created for enjoyment. Want to hang out with your friends, but it's raining and you don't want to play board games or watch movies? Here, take a whiff of this Lysergic Phlox! Nervous about a job interview or a big presentation? Take five and clear your head with a Lorazepam-rose! Kenji didn't want to relax or merely share a wonderful experience with friends, no. Kenji *wanted* to hate. Kenji *wanted* to *really* feel unrestrained loathing toward his superior.

Kenji got off of the People-Mover headed towards Assistant's Row and strode to the platform that would take him to Izakaya Town, commonly referred to as the Booze District. This area was very well guarded and regulated as alcohol had become the only intoxicant on the premises to be deemed 'inducing.' Something about communal drinking really brought out the crazy in nearly all of the staff on site. All staff and their families on-site had their own private narcogardens and a generous daily allotment of uppers, downers, psychedelics et al., and yet, everyone was relatively happy and attentive to their work. Those few who relegated themselves to only ingesting alcohol for chemical relief more often than not found themselves at odds with their coworkers. Kenji and several dozen others in the research department had taken to calling those who only drank Relics, as they were the sole staff members who would chide and scoff at narcoplants. The alcoholists, Relics of the Past, viewed their methods as traditional, proper. *Dry out your mind and body with this poison waste-water diuretic from microscopic animals that belched the fizz you're sucking down...* Kenji thought acidly, his ego keeping him aloof as to the bitter irony that he himself was headed straight for a bar stool.

Sitting at the broad wooden serving area, Kenji signaled the bartender. The man in suspenders, tall white and mustachioed, strolled over and took his order. Kenji began to order a round of Jell-O shots for himself, a college favorite, but instead started with what he drank during his PhD defense: a shot of single malt Islay Scotch with a hefeweizen back.

One down.

Kenji at first recoiled at the distillation now setting his esophagus on fire. The others in the bar took subtle notice, but right now, Kenji didn't care. Straightening himself, Kenji gulped down the cloudy wheat beer. The golden crispness and effervescent clean feeling took over his mouth. Kenji felt his shoulders relax as well as his forehead. He ordered another round.

This time Kenji stared for a moment at the Scotch. His eyes floated upward to take in the bottles behind the bar. His first round of booze turned the key that enabled him to finally shift his focus outward. Kenji noticed the bottle of 30-year old Yamizaki whiskey from Japan. He softly tore his eyes from the gleaming bottle and looked around. He caught the bartender talking to a plump Spanish woman from the cafetorium and hurriedly dumped the cheap Islay in his glass behind the bar. No one heard the little splash of liquid hitting the rubber mats and tile below. After guzzling the beer, in a bid to show he was ready for another, Kenji signaled the bartender once more.

"Excuse me, why wasn't I notified of the Japanese whiskey there?" Kenji's tongue was loose and he had planned on letting it go completely.

"Hey buddy, truth is, you didn't ask, alright?" The bartender was an old pro. He assured himself that he could always spot a greenhorn in his midst.

"Well as much as *we're* paying *you* to serve *us*... it should've been your first recommendation! I would like three fingers of the Yamizaki there. Neat."

"You're a funny guy..." The bartender leaned in to read Kenji's name patch on his right sleeve. "Kenji, you're *real* funny, you know that?" A jackal's smile refused to leave the man's face. The round little Spanish woman on the stool was blushing at the bartenders brashness.

"Just give me the damn whiskey." Kenji hung his head as he viewed this attempt at intimidation as a failure. The bartender took his time pouring the shots. The brown liquor seemed to take notice and it became unctuous in the way it left the bottle. The syrupy imported alcohol quivered as it filled each of the shot glasses that were lined them up in front of him.

"Now don't go too fast on these. It's for your own good. Hell, *I* don't even drink this poison. Look at that janitor over there. He's here every night. Poor sap." The bartender indicated a very afflicted-looking Relic. The white man, unshaven and forlorn, was staring at the same plump Spanish woman the bartender had been talking to. "Yeah, she was his partner for a time, but he just couldn't put the booze down. Still can't."

"So why's he here then?"

"Because when he drinks, he gets all... sad. And mopey. He's older, so instead of just, I don't know, *learning something new*, he chooses to fear the narcoplants. Doesn't actually *want* to get better, y'know? Because if he gets better, then more will be expected and ultimately he'll have to do more work. At least that's how he tells it."

"Pssh... Relics... all born and bred when fear was still the only method of governmental control..." Kenji's tongue was loosening further.

"What was that?" The bartender, young and smart as he looked, had apparently not heard of the Senator Omar Cortez (D-CA) Fear Doctrine. This was a protocol, exposed in the form of inter-departmental memos, that authorized and directed the usage of the single most powerful tool wielded by the proverbial powers-that-be: fear. When the public was made aware of the manipulation coming directly from Congress, a Tea-Party-esque uprising occurred and a purge of the legislature took place. New laws replaced the old. Many non-violent convictions were overturned, records expunged. The old alcoholist Relic janitor, with his push broom moustache and sideburns, bore all the marks of someone born too soon to benefit from the freedom that the exposure of the Cortez Doctrine provided. Inspired by the actions of the American people, millions of other people the world over moved to free themselves from the shackles of fear mongering tactics employed in nearly every human-led government. The only real downside to all of this was that, with the plebeian class no longer easily controllable, the old ruling classes felt exceedingly vulnerable. Thus, an old fear was dug up and resurrected: a repeat of the French Revolution.

The UN had, of course, taken note of the sudden mass awakening and had, of course, taken the steps necessary in order to keep a close eye on the governments of the world and their ability to keep their citizens in check.

His eyes weary and dull, the alcoholist Relic took a final, sloppy swig of his yeast-born toxin. He clumsily wiped his mouth and jerked his block-shaped head to gawk at the voluptuous, overflowing Spanish woman at the corner of the bar. She was once more engaged in deep conversation with the bartender.

"You.... Y-you get your filthee lipsh away from her!" *Belch* "Coward!"

The Relic's outburst had gotten the full attention of the bar.

"That there... th-that woman... issss mine!" He hurled the accusation along with his finger at the strapping bartender.

"Hey look pal, if she wants to talk with me, she's an adult and she can do as she pleases. Now I've told you before, *Jerry*, if you're gonna keep comin' in here and harassing my customers, I'll put you on the *list!* Are we clear, *Jerry*?"

Jerry had passed out.

Kenji shook his head in disapproval. *If you're going to get drunk, do it at home, or at least have enough sense to not embarrass yourself,* Kenji thought.

With the portly señorita now shaking her head, the bartender and another worker bee drug the Relic outside and called for a transport to return him to his dorm.

Kenji now took his last finger of Yamizaki and knocked it back. Orange-based citrus notes accented the robust burnt-barrel taste that engulfed his senses.

"Say, you're not lookin' to end up like ole Jerry there are ya?" The bartender inquired.

With absolute seriousness, Kenji mustered his boldest facial expression. His left eye popped while his right eye squinted. His nostrils flared in syncopation with the grinding of his teeth. His ear waggled. His eyebrows rollicked into a sudden dagger.

"Of course not…" Was all he could manage.

Kenji Hirasawa awoke the following day on the floor of his office, in his manor on Assistant's Row. All around him lay the various contents of his file cabinets. His head weighed a thousand pounds. Kenji opened and shut his dry and filmed-over mouth, slowly climbed to his feet, and tried to remember what happened. He puttered around the piles of papers, kicking things here and there. He winced and rubbed the back of his neck with each failed memory. The degrees and plaques on his wall regarded him with stale mocking.

Kenji, furious with his faulty memory, burst out into his own personal narcogarden. Quickly locating an amphetdrangea, he zealously ripped the flower from its spot in the earth and greedily began rubbing the plant all over his face. The skin on his cheeks began to tingle and feel better than normal. His energy level rose, as did his mood. Within a few minutes his head weighed what he felt it ought to, and he could now clearly recall the previous evening's events properly.

Kenji arrived home after a brief stop at another bar in the accountants district. Not long after he walked in the door, he let go of his self control and began to treat his own work as he felt Dr. Endo viewed it, like garbage. Years of research and study had been defaced, deorganized, and wildly strewn about. In the back of his mind Kenji beat himself up only briefly as there were, of course, highly organized digital copies of everything.

These original hardcopies though... There was

something to actually owning the physical manifestation of one's life work, no matter how many backups there were. These were papers he himself wrote notes on. The documents he himself prepared and signed off on.

Like the drinking, it was done to torture himself, he reasoned.

Endlessly torturing myself, he thought. *That means I'm no better than Larry, or Jerry, whatever that alcoholist Relic's name was.*

Kenji started to clean up and reorganize his things, but a third of the way through, he stopped. Focusing on his hands, Kenji was mentally walked through every attempt to show Endo, his previous boss Tsuguhiko Noda, and even his own father something he made. Something Kenji spent real time on. No one cared to see it. Everyone in Kenji's life saw him as a vehicle through which their own dreams could be realized, *Kenji be damned!*

At last he grew fed up with his own circular thinking. When he did, Kenji caught sight of the time.

He was two hours late for work.

He felt a weight settle on his shoulders. Kenji flash-panicked for a few minutes. In a feverish running through his manor, he took a three minute shower, stuffed a few rice balls in his face, and as he was putting on a clean lab coat, he saw himself in the mirror.

There he is... A voice within him started. *Like a good little doggy, the number two of this whole operation comes when he's called...*

Kenji spit his ID badge from his mouth, crumpled up his fresh clothing and hurled it into a corner. He tock a steadying deep breath before making his next move. Kenji walked over to the standard wall-mounted interface and tapped the icon on the screen indicating he was taking a personal day. The higher members of staff were to be given fourteen of these a year, to be used whenever the hard working doctors and scientists simply needed a break. Until this point in his career, Kenji had never taken personal time like this. Of course like all humans, Kenji got sick from time to time, but with his being the first of a new breed of geneticists, Kenji had modified his own genome in a bid to combat illness. So far, though, he had only made it very easy for him to mask the symptoms of a viral illness.

With his alibi in place, Kenji now put on a casual, concealing yet inconspicuous, set of clothing. He did not want anyone to notice him and what he was about to do.

Kenji called for a driverless transport wearing a long brown coat and a porkpie hat with sunglasses. The small, comfortable, electric unicycle appeared and Kenji, employing a gruff and impersonal tone, immediately ordered the vocal recognition feature disabled. He then manually programmed the route he wished it to take and set off. Kenji was whisked through nearly every bit of vivacious scenery that life immediately outside the black nest could offer. He took the long way and cruised around the cricket field, through the botanical gardens, and back around past the row of the residence blocks until he had arrived.

Amongst those not in management, word had spread of a black market shop hidden in plain sight in the residence block that housed the cafetorium kitchen staff. Kenji took the long way there as, being someone in management, he could not afford to be seen patronizing the black market shop. The worker-bee-class called it 'black market' simply because it sold alcohol with the intent of the purchaser *taking it home.* While this was perfectly acceptable behavior outside of Warren G. Harding ATSP, inside it was considered in the same light as human trafficking. Narcoplants provided enriching communal activity and individual enlightenment, whereas alcohol in the home could more so lead to anger, depression, isolation, rue, violence, and loss of productivity, all of which could destabilize the environment carefully crafted within the walls of Warren G. Harding, ATSP. All this according to the plethora of "Wellness Reminders" that blanketed the walls and stairwells of the facility like Tokyo subway ads.

Kenji adroitly crept along from apartment to apartment. He arrived at what should be apartment 9, but was greeted by a second apartment 6. He checked his trail, and noticed that, yes, this very door should have a 9 nailed to it. *Nailed to it.* He then noticed a nail *missing*, thus causing the mass-produced brass number to hang in response, rendering it a mere 6.

The contractors had been told to skimp on the worker-bee-class dorms near the airstrip as the dwellings and their tenants had not been deemed 'mission critical'. This despite their highly essential function of harvesting and preparing edible foodstuffs for the convicted felons, who were to be unaware of their collective being experimented on. A memo from Butch Cairns had advocated for an autonomous feeding apparatus, but the board of directors for TASC explicitly stated that there was to be human-powered agriculture and culinary answers for the questions relating to the feeding of inmate-patients.

Kenji gave the secret knock: three quick taps from the left hand, followed by a paradiddle.

The door opened a crack and gravelly voice slithered out, "Yeah?"

Kenji, doing his best to remain cool responded, "Yamizaki?"

The voice grumbled various racially charged insults until Kenji slid several hundred dollars through the quickly closing opening in the door. The voice ceased profaning once the amount had been fully counted.

After a time, the voice returned. "Go around the corner and reach into the hedge under the banana trees. You may return five more times, at this exact time, to the same spot in the hedges. Failure to do so with utmost punctuality will results in your lifetime ban. Thank you. I'm sorry, Arigatou."

Kenji made scrupulous note of the time. It was just after 1130am. With a brisk calmness he turned the corner and caught sight of the banana tree. He scouted the area. It was a beautiful day and there were recreators everywhere. The banana tree was encircled by a robust hedge, as were all the other banana trees in this unifying plaza. The banana tree closest to him sported a garbage disposal furnace. A woman, clearly a department head, mindlessly hucked an unfinished ice cream in the general direction of the small fusion-powered device. The ice cream cone missed. Kenji seized the opportunity and scurried over to clean up her mess. He smiled, knelt down, and quickly shot his hand into the shrubbery. He stood, and while smoothly placing the fallen cone into the repository, he slid out a slender shoebox from the growth. In one motion, the cone went into the rubbish, the box went into his coat. Easy as that.

Once more Kenji summoned a transport and programmed it to take him to the entry plaza of Assistant's Row; he would walk the rest of the way to avoid suspicion. He peeked inside the box as the machine whirred while shuttling him home. He saw the caramel-colored elixir straight away and quickly resealed the box.

Kenji dismissed the craft, and trotted up the stairs to his doorway. Taking the elevator made him too exposed. When he reached his floor, he looked down the hallway. Empty, as it should be at this time of day. He blinked into his doorway and immediately drew all the blinds on his balcony. His comm device was still in the drawer next to his bed. No new messages. He set the small shoebox on his kitchen counter and retrieved a crystal glass. Carefully opening the box, Kenji removed the sealant from around the cork and gently worked it loose. He brought the bottle to his nose and inhaled the spicy aroma. The pour from bottle to glass was almost arousing.

His mouth watering, Kenji raised the glass and rested it on his bottom lip.

To me, he thought.

"That Kenji..." Dr. Yoshida Endo shook his head in disapproval. "Did he really think we didn't know about the speakeasy? Maybe I should have let him show me his work... Too late now." Dr. Endo walked away from the monitor and turned his attention to the vast arrangement of two-way stained-glass that made up the ceiling of the Cafetorium.

30 Days Before Unity

Warren G. Harding ATSP

It was 1220pm.

Lunchtime.

Atherton Mars and his closest all sat in a bunch near the south exit. Stanton Finch and a sprinkling of his racist cohorts spoke in hushed tones near the north exit. Tito Manzanas ate from a bowl, hands-free, while surrounded by his most loyal followers. Desmond Cavendish and the rest of his all waited for their man in the kitchen to come join them.

The other inmate-patients all lined up in the same place, regardless of coverall color, and received their meals from the same series of windows carved into a concrete wall, regardless of the dish. Window 1 gave vegetables, Window 2 gave a starch, Window 3 gave a protein, and Window 4 gave a desert. Today, though, Window 4 doled out a new desert: a small Jell-O shot that sparkled. Each inmate received one with their meal, in addition to a small card that read: EAT ME FIRST! On the reverse there was a promise of more sweets for all who ate their Jell-O in front of the guard at the end of the line.

The first to eat were the Oranges. It was just better for everyone that way. The Reds came in next and would sit down just as the Oranges began to leave. Next were the

Blues, and lastly the Green psionic inmates. This lunch phasing was designed to keep the inmates from cross pollenating abilities, corroborating theories, and any other undesired social activity ala gang formation and its subsequent warfare.

Desmond's Black Leather Crows, The Red Sons of Stanton, Los Animales Rabiosas Naranjas, and The Green Hindu Frankenstein all existed in spite of the anti-gang protocols. When the inmates began to poke at the walls of WGH:ATSP they found ways to intermingle with cohorts and the like. Sock message was the most popular and effective method of gang creation. These men, wayward to society as they were, were not stupid, or ignorant individuals. The more pushback they got for secretly uniting, the deeper their ties bonded.

When the TASC appointed Executive Chef of WGH:ATSP Inmate Cafetorium was approached, two days into Project Phlea Circus, and told to start adding strange liquids, powders, and granules from unmarked, yet colored, canisters to the food, he resigned on the spot. He insisted on knowing what every atom entering his kitchen was and what dish it was meant for. After his compensation was adjusted to a number much, much higher than what he jokingly stipulated in his demands for retention, he acquiesced, with one condition: certain well-behaved inmates must be allowed to perform janitorial duties in his kitchen.

The Chef had ran a cruise ship kitchen before, and the work-study program made him feel generous and benevolent. Given that this was a prison, hidden in **[LOCATION REDACTED]**, the entire situation being very similar to cooking on a cruise ship, he missed that old feeling of helping out a ne'er do well.

TASC cautiously agreed, and had their on-site engineering outfit fabricate a sort of 'janitorial bubble suit', created ostensibly for "exposure to caustic chemicals and general inmate safety". This new construct would house these "well behaved and upstanding inmates of both good example and deportment" in a boy-in-a-bubble situation. The inmates could sweep and perform other laborious kitchen tasks without hearing or seeing a thing. Inside the orbital and encompassing helmet were screens and speakers, all designed to project what the Lord Warden saw fit to project for them. Most of the time they saw merely a kitchen with black blobs representing other people. The prep tables and spice shelves were covered in blurred pixels, but things like organic cleaner and the mop bucket shone in crystal clear high-definition.

On this day, of all days, an inmate in the work-study janitorial program, the Black Leather Crow Desmond was waiting for, got tired of his shift and faked a myocardial infarction for kicks. His actions wound up consuming just enough time to throw off the seating rhythm. The guards, without the doctors present, due to a rare and impromptu safety meeting, saw only their rotational schedules, and allowed the majority of Blues and Reds, with a smattering of Greens and less than a handful of slow-eating Oranges, to all sit down and eat together. The kitchen ground to a halt in order to tend to the now-flailing, weak, man.

"Hurry it up!" Viktor Tandy barked at the inmates. He didn't like what was happening in the kitchen. He hated what was happening in the Cafetorium.

"Nope! This was a mistake! Everybody up!" Viktor Tandy was not about to listen a panel of Japanese tear him to shreds for this decision.

"No way!" Shouted a Blue.

"I'm starving and I just sat down!" Yelled a Red.

"Not my problem! Up! NOW!" Viktor drew his weapon.

This, was also a mistake.

Viktor Tandy winced as a plastic lunch tray collided with his skull.

"WHITE POWER!" A Red Son of Stanton stood and erupted before jamming his entire fist down the throat of the nearest Blue, a Leather Crow named Quincy Coleman-Cypress. Tito Manzanas roared and avenged Quincy, in a gruesome, wet, and noisy fashion. Several nearby inmates vomited in response.

Viktor Tandy tried to fight the inmate who initially struck him, but fell unconscious after having his head smashed together with a pale-skinned Red.

The fight was on.

Inmates used their own bodies to clog up the entryways and exits. Tribal warfare exploded as the inmates scrambled about, seeking both enemy and ally.

The fighting took a turn for the brutal.

A clutch of Oranges, led by Tito Manzanas, clicked and whooped as they preyed on others with their jagged and broken teeth.

Then, all at once, each inmate suddenly began to experience wild and profane hallucinations.

Blues were fighting anything and everything, with no clear loyalty. Reds broke into clusters and tried to get into the kitchen, their ultimate goal the foodstuffs in the kitchen area. The rest of the mass of hatred and repression was comprised of Greens and Oranges, all using their minds against all others.

Atherton Mars caused several inmates' immediate nosebleeds, deafness, and eventually cardiac cessation.

"This is it, boys!" Atherton roared, his eyes blazing.

Truly, each faction believed, via the effects of TASC-brand Amplified reality combined with a potent dose of Hirasawa-brand psilocybin, that this brawl was their entire raison d'etre.

"Spyder!" A random and idle Yellow shrieked in abject fear.

The lone real correctional robot descended into the fray. It was quickly subdued and torn to pieces by several multi-colored inmates. The loose parts of the deconstructed machine were ripped from the chassis and used as weapons.

"Where're all the other Spyders?" A guard barked at no one. The holograms posing as real Spyders all did nothing, as they were no more than projected light. "The other ones aren't even moving!"

Only Endo, and a select few others knew the truth, of course.

From the other side of the two-way ceiling, Endo calmly watched the mayhem. The majority of the inmates were in the cafetorium. The rest were in their cells. To him, the entire incident was neatly contained. He sipped a handless mug of green tea while another cord of guards approached the fight scene. Endo took his eyes from the fight and glanced at the four-dimensional, holographic, map of the cells at-large. He noticed the inmate registered to the address of #BB1123RHW hadn't moved for quite some time, despite the ruckus. The others' still in their cells were at least pacing or doing rudimentary calisthenics to get rid of the vibe that was swelling in the food place. He enlarged the cell and focused intently on the frozen dot. Just as he moved to call a Dorm-Level guard off of his post to go and check on inmate #BB1123RHW, the dot began erratically circling the cell. At first, Endo thought the movements random and odd, but after several seconds, he could make out a pattern, and decided to return his attention to the mayhem at hand. He sipped from his mug and smiled as the guards at last overcame one of the blockages made of bodies and had begun pouring into the cafetorium proper.

Desmond, ducking and rolling away from the main fracas, managed to walk right past the guards who had punctured their way through the mass of flesh. They were streaming into the cafetorium to bring order to the heinous chaos and simply ignored anything going in the opposite direction. Desmond happened upon a sleeping doctor nestled comfortably in an on-call room. He took off the sock on his left foot, balled it up and jammed it into the mouth of the doctor. The doctor woke and tried a defense, but Desmond's fist arrested any attempt of upheaval.

Desmond, now wearing the scrubs and keycard of the fallen doctor, made his way to the dorms that the deposed practitioner lived in. Once inside, he rifled through the items searching for anything of use. He moved into the bedroom and discovered the doctor's spouse. She was asleep on the bed, her face shown snow white, her perfect lips barely parted, he stood for a moment watching her breathe. Desmond Cavendish looked around and gambled on the dresser holding a something, anything, of value. He crept over to the dresser and carefully slid the top drawer open. Under the layers of socks and t-shirts his hand hit something semi-hard, round. Lifting it up, his jaw came loose and hung. A wad of American silver-bills. He counted quickly, over $10,000 in silver notes. Hearing her stir, he bounded in silence out of the room and towards the door. Sleepily the woman muttered something in Japanese just as the hulking Black inmate softly shut the front door.

Desmond Cavendish was outside of the residence and in dire need of a way out and off of the grounds of Warren G. Harding ATSP. At a self-sustaining facility, traffic *never* came and went, though.

The sun was entering the third quarter of the day and Desmond then realized he had no idea *where* he was. When they transferred him from Sing Sing, they never said aloud the exact locale he was headed to.

Desmond gazed out at the landscape. He took in the flatiron-shaped mountains, the blueness of the sky, beyond the fence was tall grass… Plainsgrass! I must be in the middle of the country, he thought, somewhere around Colorado or Wyoming, maybe even Nebraska.

Noise, coming closer. Desmond scurried around to a bloom of plants that capped the aisles of the doctor's dorms. He leapt in and encased himself in the thick botanical shrouds. Two whole regiments of guards, in full riot gear, trudged past him headed for the cafetorium. Things were getting serious in there.

Desmond Cavendish sensed it was safe and emerged from the bloom. He dashed towards the border of the facility, having resolved that he was just going to walk out of here after all. After some deft navigation, Desmond approached a decorative part of the fence. He realized that he had never seen this part of the facility before. The topiaries and bonsai displays intrigued him. More noise, this time from down a nearby path. Desmond now engulfed himself in a topiary carved to resemble President Pickford De La Croix. Several guards, Praetorian-class, ambled up the garden path. *Where am I?*

Desmond thought on. *Why have I never heard of this building and its gardens?* The guards marched past the topiary and up to the front door of a Victorian estate. The door flung open and a large Black man in a yukata and geta hurried them inside. *The Lord Warden perhaps?*

The area was once again devoid of human life. Desmond emerged from the botany and progressed towards the edge of the garden. Here he noticed the complete lack of electric fencing. In fact, the complete lack of fencing of any kind, save the hedge and bamboo lining the rear of the grounds. Seizing the moment, Desmond Cavendish dove over the hedge and rolled through the small bamboo grove.

Desmond now rolled down a short hillside and came to a stop at a stream. He checked his pockets and made sure the silver notes were still there. His attention now turned to orientating himself and finding his way back to his wife. His *real* wife. By now, he had remembered everything. The fury of being tricked by those once over him served as fuel for his desire to hold his beautiful Alice again. *This time is different. This time I wont even look at a bottle. Alice is my queen*, he said to himself, *and I will treat her as such.*

Looking to sky, he made note of the sun's position with his hand and gathered he would be heading south if he followed the stream. After all, it had to go somewhere.

Desmond walked for several hours. Not once did he come across a sign of human activity of any kind. The stream wound and slid neatly across the countryside.

Night descended, and Desmond was exhausted. Noticing a small cluster of plains cottonwood trees,

Desmond snapped off a few branches and fashioned a rudimentary shelter. He then dug a Dakota fire pit and made camp.

As he sat by the near-invisible fire, a thought occurred to him: *Do I have a tracking chip in me somewhere?* The truth was that he did not. Yes, the doctors and guards said they put one in him. Yes, he had a small incision scar on his right wrist. Yes, that had all been a lie to allay many of the more expensive fears the De La Croix administration had raised. Many of the Security Features and Measures detailed to the American Half of Project Phlea Circus existed in written word only. Things like facial recognition and live-DNA monitoring were touted and demoed, but none of it was ever actually implemented. TASC was trying to turn some sort of profit, after all.

Ignorant to the fakery he had endured, Desmond sourced a nearby sharp rock and dug into the tiny scar on his right wrist. The wound yielded only pain.

The following morning, Desmond Cavendish was woken by the sound of mating. He Peered out from inside his cottonwood micro-hut. Desmond saw a bull and several cows all enjoying the natural process of procreation. *I'm on a farm! People! But what about my clothes? What do I say I was doing here? Where did I come from?* Then it hit him.

Desmond emerged from his shelter and scouted the grounds. He saw, at about 200 meters off, a rusted barb-wire fence. Beyond that, a road. Desmond, striding with the absolute confidence of a man who belonged on the steer grounds, made his way toward the fence.

As he attempted to traverse the neglected barrier, his scrubs got caught. As he tugged on them he could hear tearing. *I'm stuck! No, trapped!* Desmond's thoughts raced as to what this could imply were he caught.

Suddenly, a voice.

"Hey! You there!"

Dammit! He screamed internally.

"Hey! What's that matter? You stuck?" the voice came with a semi-taunting tone. Soon a redneck-looking fellow and a young child made their way over to Desmond.

"Well, lookie here Bobby, looks like we caught something." The farmer and his son approached with caution. Desmond's idea was about to be put to the test.

"Can I help you sir? Or shall I just rustle up some of my stock and let you waltz out of here with it?" The redneck said accusingly.

"Hehe, no I'm not here for cattle." Desmond tried to sound as natural as possible. "Actually, I'm embarrassed about the situation I'm in."

"Hell, I would be too. Caught 'nappin' cattle red handed."

"I told you I'm not here for *cattle*. I have this… condition."

"Condition?"

"Yes. Every now and then I enter something called a fugue state. Do you know what that is?"

"Shoot, naw."

"I do daddy." The boy now speaks.

"Well, what is it, Bobby?"

"It's when stress or somethin' makes you so crazy

you black out and wake up somewhere else." The boy dolefully looked at his father.

"He's absolutely right. My wife and I have it out sometimes and that, combined with my medical profession," he gestured at his attire. "Can lead to oft damaging psychological effects."

"I see..." said the farmer. "And one of these few-guh states happened, and here you are?"

"Exactly. Now if you could just help me loose myself, I will be on my way to the local busport."

"Well, I've got too much going on 'round here to care much longer so sure, Mr... Onogawa."

"Onogawa?" Desmond said, puzzled.

"Yeah, that is yer last name ain't it? That's what's on your coat... Maybe he's still in it, Bobby?"

"Oh, yeah, sorry, just not used to hearing it outside of the hospital."

"Mm hmm, well I kept my last name when I got married, but to each his own."

With that the redneck loosed Desmond from the fence and pointed him in the direction of the busport. When he was a few yards away, Desmond turned back, cupped his hands around his mouth and shouted "Say, where am I?" The redneck laughed and shouted back "Why you're on the outskirts of Wareland, Colorado!"

Wareland, Colorado.

Desmond shook his head as he continued down the road, towards the eventual town of Wareland itself.

Upon reaching the busport is downtown Wareland Colorado, Desmond Cavendish purchased a one-way ticket for himself to head back east, to Alice. Desmond stopped at a clothiers and used some of the silver dollars to buy a new outfit on his way into town. The cashier regarded the notes, as they were still getting used to the Gold and Silver standard.

"Say, how'd you come across the large denominations? I only ask cuz I've got some personal business and the silver coins are just too many…" The cashier trailed off.

"Oh, uh," Desmond worked to manufacture a response. "I just went to the bank and asked," he said the first common-sense thing that came to his mind.

"Well, I guess I *could* just go do that. Problem is the bank manager is the person I've got to square up with…"

Desmond paid the man, smiled, and wished him good luck on his way out the door.

He dumped the doctor's clothes and ID into a dumpster that was painted bright pink. This flagged the dumpster as one that would be taken directly to the town incinerator where it would be converted into energy, thus erasing his connection to Warren G. Harding.

His bus took off at 1445pm and arrived in Brooklyn at 0715am, the next day. Desmond cut his way through the crowds, navigating the old city with expert precision. He arrived at his old brownstone at 0900am, and stood at the base of the stoop. His old Venusian rosebush seemed to acknowledge him, in its own way, and greeted him. The flowers grew out of a planter Desmond had kept up in secret, hiding in plain sight not ten feet from the door to the apartment complex. He was relieved to see the flowers thriving despite his months-long absence. Desmond reached out to grab a buxom flower and took a deep breath, inhaling the intoxicating scent of the lush speckled rose in his hands. Climbing each step felt like summiting a mountain peak. First, Mt. Baldy, then Denali, then Kilimanjaro. The stoop was conquered, but the doorbell remained. Some would describe it as their Everest, Desmond saw it as his Olympus Mons. Extending a digit, Desmond depressed the ersatz rubber button, completing the circuit and sending the necessary electrons hurtling towards the bell inside Alice' apartment. Her voice came on the intercom.

"Yes?"

Silence.

"Hello? Who's there? The vidfeed is broken and the Super can't be bothered to fix it, who is it?"

Desmond mustered up all he had, and opened his mouth. "Hi Ali," Was all he could manage.

Silence.

"Alice, honey, sweetheart, it's…" His voice wavered. "It's me. Desmond."

"Desmond… What, what are you doing here? How did you…"

"Baby, we need to talk. Just please, trust me. I… I need you. I-I-I love you."

Silence.

After an interval, the door buzzed open. Desmond

cursed the broken elevator and bounded up the stairs. Once at her door, the cleanest one on the floor, he made sure his clothes were tidy looking and the roses he plucked from the doorway were still perky.

He knocked.

She opened.

He entered.

Locking the door, Alice turned to reveal she had been crying. Her porcelain skin almost seemed to glow.

"I brought you these."

"Desmond…" she marveled at the plants, taking in their esters, letting her nose indulge. "Desmond these are *Venusian!* How could you afford these?"

"Don't worry about that baby," he said. Desmond never told her where the roses he cared for near their stoop had really come from. He never told her that when he stole, he stole to make her life richer. "Just know that I've had considerable time to think and time to come to appreciate what it means to have your world taken from you. Alice, I love you. With all my heart. In fact, I even had something done while inside. Look."

Desmond showed her his hand. On his left ring finger was a crude tattoo of her name and the date they had set for their wedding, which never happened. Tears began streaming from her eyes. The flowers fell to the carpet as the two lovers embraced.

"Desmond I swear to God if you touch another bottle…"

"Shhh…baby I'm back. I will be dry from now until I die. I love *you.* I came here for *you.* I am not going to put anything between us again. You and me baby. You & me."

Three weeks later, Alice rose from the couch to get a coat as the two were finally ready to head down to the family friend/magistrate for a quick wedding. As she did, the TV wall roared to life.

BREAKING NEWS: Large, possibly nuclear explosion…

After exchanging puzzled looks, the two hurried out the door and on to their repaired life together.

Ten

complication

3 Months Before Unity

Nashville, Tennessee

The Hooters in Nashville was empty on this particular cloudy Tuesday. The Oil Riots were dominating the news cycle and, frankly, not that many people were interested in cheap beer and fried pickles at the moment. Mindy Jacsz lightly bounced as she strode in from her driverless cab and into the establishment. Mindy was 23, blonde and curvaceous. Her teeth were perfect and so was her path in life, despite losing an uncle and her brother to the Roughneck Uprising in the Gulf. After her time spent as captain of the Lady Vols Badminton team, she was taking a break and making some cash on the side at Hooters, gearing up for her anthropology trip to the Amazon to study an indigenous people with unusual birthmarks where their fingerprints should be. She was top of her class and was also pursuing a minor in crypto-linguistics.

Pavel Stënk had been born to Russian parents in the nascent New Austria-Hungary, and was more recognizable as Pavel the Lamprey. He awoke in his Viennese prison cell at 0627am and began his yoga. His space was a wild pink and yellow zebra pattern, punishment for beating a guard with a lunch tray. He pulled his leg behind his head and thought of when he did taxidermy with his father in Bucharest, when an old familiar smell crept into his cell.

Almonds, he thought to himself, *and sunshine…*

Mindy opened the restaurant at 1300pm. At 1303pm a poorly bearded Pavel the Lamprey stumbled into the restaurant and collapsed, his arms tied to his sides, and his fingers glued together into flippers. He was 'holding' a note. Eager to help a stranger, Mindy dove over the bar counter (all five-feet-four-inches of her) and cop-rolled to his side.

"Sir, I say, sir!" Mindy shook Pavel while noticing the letters tattooed onto his ring, middle and index finger knuckles: OLM OMD.

"ARE YOU OK?" She monotonously, loudly, talked at him.

"Hmmmph-hrrmph hmmmph hmm," his mouth was not only obstructed by a crudely glued on and lengthy white beard, it was also clogged with a dirty old sock. Pavel writhed on the floor and a crumpled bloody note floated out of his gooey cuffed hands and into hers, it read:

"Dear Mindy, my name is Pavel and I love you. I love you more than anything I could ever imagine. I have watched you daily as you arrive and set up this restaurant to be filled with your laughter and very large tips. That is why I have chosen to blow us up, so that we may inherit the rich and satisfying blessings of the sacred and blessed messenger of Allah, peace be upon him, Charles Darwin..."

The note rambled on speaking of the misplaced glory surrounding Charles Darwin. Not only that, the note declared that in order to truly care for the Earth as an evolved human, one must find a way to kill off as many fellow humans lacking any desirable traits (as defined by the current society-at-large) *as possible*; all done in order to lighten the load of the rest still living. One less mouth, one more day.

Mindy was beside herself. She leapt to the holophone behind the bar and called the new Amplified police, as this situation was a bit too much for civilian-level Old Bill, she reasoned. The cruisers hovered down in a matter of seconds and surrounded the building.

The scanbots lingered like a cloud of gnats, craving direction from the ice-eyed, red haired commander, Jonah Tib. Jonah sneezed and the scanbots reflexed, reacting to the expulsion of mucous. "Damn this cold, scanbot swarm α17, scan me for antibodybots." He stuck his arms out and the swarm engulfed him for 2.8 seconds and rebounded.

"Scan Complete." The multi-leveled voice droned. "Scan finds ZERO antibodybots."

"Aw hell, Alikhan! Where is Alikhan?!"

Sukhvinder Fateh Alikhan appeared. He was the squad shaman and his patented antibodybots had been keeping the bastard child of AIDS and H27N14 (or Shiva as they called it in British North Western India) at bay.

The rain picked up.

"Siddartha Gautama Buddha, it's about time you showed up Sukh." Jonah's eyes shifted from ice blue to a soothing periwinkle.

"Many apologies Tib, but with the rain and the wife, things have been a bit pear-shaped as of late." He stuck him with his innocupistol and sent thousands of Shiva killing nanobots into the Commander's organic circuitry. The bots identified and consumed the Shiva. They were intricate, concise and exacting. However, this Shiva virus was telepathic and could piggyback onto a human's natural beta brainwaves and actually talk with other infected in the area. The Ultranet even had rumors that a virile Shiva host can signal others nearby whose infection is dormant and initiate infection if need be. Shiva was not to be taken lightly.

"I swear to Buddha I can feel them crawling in my body Sukh, WOOO! So what'd'we have here?" Jonah pulled out his holostik and projected a nine-inch screen into the wet air in front of him. The holoscreen showed Pavel on the floor of the restaurant, Mindy behind the bar and a deformity on Pavel's stomach. "Swarm, scan the gentleman on the floor for explosives." The cloud of bots took to the restaurant and beamed back an MRI of the man's midsection. Just to the left of his stomach, behind his duodenum was a small thermo-nuclear biological bomb, the new model Sweet Susan that the Russian Federation had developed to keep Scotland from wresting control of sub-Saharan Africa out of their Vodka-soaked hands.

"Alright boys we got us a Russo-Austro-Hungarian

loon and it looks like he's had a Sweet Susan for lunch. I want a polyhex dome over the 'straunt, Nagasaki strength," he bellowed all of this to his loyal task force. "I need a creeper, and do we have any psionic's on hand? Is anyone here a psi? No? Ok, then get me that creeper, ASAP!"

An Amplified biologist ran up with a small, clear cylindrical aquarium. He set it down next to Commander Jonah Tib and removed the odd mason jar lid. An orange and green pulsing ball of blue and yellow veins oozed out of the jar and formed a crude face. The three eyes locked onto Jonah who then issued several distinct telepathic commands. The creature acknowledged the directions, then melted into the soggy ground. All eyes present fixed themselves onto the Hooters with eager anticipation. The dome was lowered at an eighteen-degree slope, leaving room for people to walk in. The plasmacopter hovered overhead holding the dome in a panted silence, it too waiting for the creeper to act.

As Pavel lay on the ground, powerfully confused by what was happening, he heard a voice, "Hello Pavel, why are you here?" Pavel wondered the same to himself. *How* did *I get here*, he thought. *Why does my stomach hurt? Who is this woman?* The creeper fed all this to an apparatus the Amplified biologist sat at. Jonah Tib read the output and sat dumbfounded. "Hell, just spring the damn thing so we can get out of here. It's wet and we need to redeploy back at the riot zones," Jonah shook his head. The creeper apologized to the Commander before forming a large pouch around Pavel, who fainted from shock. The fleshy sack then rolled outside like an underinflated tire.

"Now what?" Sukhvinder's intrigue was snared by the sounds approaching officials.

"Hell if I know. I gotta call this guy in." Jonah Tib was then confronted by several copper haired Japanese men in white, orange, and green jumpsuits. They appeared amongst the others and surprised the entire battalion. The obvious leader, "Steve", handed Jonah Tib a letter, signed by President De La Croix and Vice President Mansfield Cairns, and Jonah's own boss, Maxwell Deng. The letter declared Pavel as the newest member of a highly volatile terrorist group, deathly committed to the survival of the fittest, indoctrinated by a deadly amalgamated corruption of Islam and Charles Darwin's famed children's book, the Origin of Species. One Less Mouth, One More Day served as their creed. Pavel the Lamprey was to immediately be sent over to the newly renovated Alcatraz prison in the 53rd state, the San Francisco Bay Area.

The next time Pavel opened his eyes, he was in a jail cell. His muscles ached. The thin mattress he found himself on creaked along with his body. His face felt strange.

Pavel raised his hand to examine further and discovered a rough and false beard affixed firmly to his face.

Hooters...

A faint memory flickered.

Charles Darwin...

"He's up!"

A gruff voice barked.

"ЧТО..." He rubbed the back of his sore head.

"Quiet!"

Pavel blinked and blinked but his eyes kept going in and out of focus. His mouth tasted like asphalt and rue.

"They couldn't get his beard off?"

"...No, apparently not. Something about the adhesive they used..." the doctor standing next to the hulking guard said from behind a clipboard.

Pavel gave his stiff and coarse 'beard' a serious tug. It was locked in place. He let out a sigh and asked for water. The guard tossed him a half-empty, rumpled, plastic water bottle. The water was stale.

"Where am I?" Pavel's rough English sounded vaguely threatening.

"That right there is classified, beard-o."

The guard and the doctor shared a laugh.

Pavel finished his dusty water and sighed.

Sunlight wafted in and alit on the bare floor.

"You fully woke yet, inmate number… 9919?"

9919? Pavel thought while he busied his hands with the water bottle.

"да, I mean, yes, I am awake now."

"Good. *The Lamprey*? What the hell?" The guard continued looking over the doctor's shoulder and onto the forms on his clipboard.

"Yes, a Lamprey is a suction eel from the deep blue sea," said Dr. Shinagawa.

"Uh huh, and why is he *that*?"

"Oh, hm. I'm, uh, I'm not quite sure…" the little doctor flipped over several pages.

"It is because I climb things without equipment. I just *stick* to buildings," Pavel answered in a non-committal way.

"Uh huh, ok. Well, my name is Walt the Guard, and as long as you're here in San Fran— shit."

"San Fran-*shit*? Where the hell is that?" Pavel was even more confused.

"That's not what I—"

"He's not supposed to know where he is!" The doctor's voice quivered.

"I know, dammit!"

"So… I'm in *Alcatraz*?" Pavel hazarded a guess.

"So far, he's the fastest to figure it out…" The little doctor wrote down several items.

"Shut up, will ya?!"

"Alcatraz…"

"You too! Shut your mouth!" The guard flailed in

his speech, working diligently to reassert his dominance.

"Now listen *Lamprey*, I don't give a damn about that beard of yours, which of course means your next stop is the showers!"

"How long have I been here?"

"This is your 62nd hour in this facility," the doctor responded.

"Two and a half days…"

"And none of it with a proper washing. Now, up!"

Pavel was incredulous.

"I said, up!"

Pavel stood.

"Good dog. Larry! Open 9919!"

A buzz echoed down the corridor, and Pavel's door slid open.

The guard cuffed Pavel, and together the three men began their march towards the bathing facilities.

As they passed other cells, Pavel noticed that the majority were empty. Those that were populated held familiar looking individuals.

Dmitri? Pavel thought as he passed another man also wearing a tacky and cheap-looking false white beard. *Kirill? Boris 'the Chimera' Teplov?* Together with himself, every other prisoner he saw ultimately comprised a Rogue's Gallery of all-star international criminals.

How did they catch all of you…

The famous hot showers of Alcatraz were certainly better than the icy tap at the gulag he had woken up in not thirty-six hours earlier.

When it was all over, his false beard remained. The skin beneath the coarse backing was beginning to itch and burn.

"Next stop, Mess Hall."

Walt the Guard led the trio to where Pavel would be eating for the foreseeable future. Already in the olive drab room was another clutch of European-looking prisoners. Each man huddled over his metal plate of food and shot looks of maniacal suspicion at the others.

"To hell with this! I am no man's Guinea Pig!" an inmate, tall and black-haired, burst to his feet and charged a guard with his metal plate in ready position.

The guard remained calm, stoic.

The man hollered and plowed forward with all his might.

The guard was motionless.

The other inmates lowered their heads, refusing to look at the scene unfolding before them.

"Last chance," the guard muttered to the shrieking man.

The inmate doubled down and picked up pace.

In one smooth motion, the guard produced a pistol and shot the man clean through his left eye. The noise echoed around the room and reverberated in the souls of every man wearing prison stripes.

The body reacted to the force of the bullet and nearly completed a half-flip.

The contents of the prisoners' skull splattered across the ceiling and rained down onto the other inmates.

No one came to remove the body.

Once more, the guard was a motionless sentry.

"Never forget!" echoed around the room as each guard in attendance took a turn firmly stating the phrase.

The words themselves were painted in bright red block letters on the south wall, along with the rest of the phrase:

we can just kill you.

"Hm, hear that 9919? *Never forget…*"

Pavel got in line for his meal.

His meal of vitamin loaf, wilted iceberg lettuce, 1% milk, and three little Italian meringue cookies went fast. What sat around on his plate until the very end of the period were a handful of pills.

"Down the hatch, 9919."

"What are they?"

"Why do you care?"

"C'mon Walt, they're multivitamins," Dr. Shinagawa answered and assured Pavel. And it was true. The pills currently on Pavel's plate were just that, multivitamins. TASC had yet to deliver the full slate of their doctors, scientists, un-tested medications, and ersatz reality, race war included. In the meantime, Genedit LTD was providing the Top Secret staff and training for New Alcatraz. Doctor Preston Shinagawa grew up in Hayward.

Pavel grumbled and took the pills.

The trio exited the Mess Hall and continued back to Pavel's cell.

"And that there completes the tour. Or at least the parts of our facility that will be of your chief concern. If you continue to be a good little doggy, we'll let you into the library, the workshop, and perhaps the art studio. But for now, Oleg The Mute and his little squeaky book cart should be 'round in the next hour or so. You done here?" Walt directed the end of his statement at the little doctor.

"Yes, I'm all set. Welcome, Pavel," the little doctor smiled, adjusted his glasses, and left with Walt the guard.

Three and a half hours later, Pavel heard squeaky revolutions approaching his cell. Ten minutes after that, a boulder of a Black man, bearing a jagged scar along his throat, arrived with a cart swollen with battered books.

"You must be Oleg…"

Oleg nodded.

"Didn't expect you to be so… *dark*…"

Oleg began to leave.

"Hey hey hey, sorry! I'm sorry my friend. I have no problem with skin color, it's just…"

Oleg pointed to his name tag.

"Yes, exactly. The name. I had a friend named Oleg and he was White as a sheet! Dumb too…"

Oleg smirked.

"Is that *The Brothers Karamezov*?"

Oleg reached for the thick tome and handed it to Pavel through the bars.

"I may be in here for a while, so why not, right?"

Oleg nodded, and then began to pull away.

"Hey, wait, wait!"

Oleg stopped.

"How long have you been in here? Is this really San Francisco?"

Oleg gave a long, hard, blink.

"That long, eh?"

Oleg nodded.

"And San Francisco? For real?"

Oleg nodded again.

"Why are we here? What is happening?"

Oleg now pointed the scar along his throat.

"Ah, I forget. My apologies."

Oleg shook it off and tried a third time to leave, but stopped all his own.

"What? What is it, Oleg?"

Oleg looked around him, and then pointed to a spot on Pavel's cell wall. The rear wall to be exact.

"What? What is there?"

Oleg pointed with force.

"What? I don't see any- "

Pavel noticed one of the bricks in the wall was not like the others.

"Why is it different?"

When he looked back, Oleg was gone. His cart squeaked and rattled at almost the other end of the cell block.

"How did he get there so fast…"

Pavel looked at the brick, then back at his book. He pondered the interaction for several minutes before he decided to read until his thoughts settled.

Dinner came and went. His first meal in New Alcatraz had apparently been 'lunch'. The food filled him up but pained his stomach regardless.

Night fell.

Pavel leaned back on his terrible mattress and cracked open his Dostoyevsky.

Outside his cell, pneumatic brakes released their tension.

"Huh?"

Pavel sat up and trained his ears towards the barred opening serving as a window in his cell.

Another release of pneumatic air.

He got to his feet and dragged his bed until it was under the opening. He got onto the top railing and was just able to peer outside.

There were docks and a small boat with supplies. Several workers were unloading items and using a forklift.

Pavel then noticed that this activity was taking place rather awkwardly at the end of the docks. He turned his head and noticed a structure of some sort dominating the majority of the small port. He couldn't see any more though, as various trees and unkempt shrubbery obstructed his view.

Then he remembered the brick.

Pavel slid his bed back to its original place and waited for the passing pair of guards to leave his cell block.

When it was clear, Pavel began to pick around the brick Oleg had deftly indicated. In a matter of minutes, the brick became loose and slid out from its socket in the wall. Pavel had a direct, brick-sized, hole to the outside world. He could see across the bay. He could see many ships waiting in the water to be unloaded. In total disbelief he tugged at the other bricks and, after some manipulation, they too slid apart. After a dozen or so bricks had grown into a pile on his left, he realized he was staring at a perfect Pavel-sized hole to the outside. He could escape if he wanted to.

Pavel crept out from his cell and found himself inside a large bush. It was impossible to see him, his hole, or his next few steps for that matter. The Eastern Bay Area greeted him. For a time, Pavel remained stationary, weighing his options.

If he left, he'd freeze in the water or get eaten by whatever currently lived in The Bay. If he stayed, well, he had no idea what would happen if he stayed. He hadn't even been conscious for 24 hours.

Stay or The Bay, stay or The Bay…

Pavel heard crying.

He crept along the wall, awash in foliage, until he arrived at another barred opening. A man, a prisoner, was crying into his cot. Pavel could make out some of the man's sobbing words.

"My precious, my love, my true one…"

Pavel decided to stay.

He slunk back towards his corruption in the facility wall and restacked the bricks. As he bundled himself into his sheet, the crying man's emotional intensity clung to Pavel's bones.

Something was very off-balance about this entire

operation, and Pavel, having only been here a short while, decided to do something, anything, about it.

To be successful though, Pavel would have to bide his time, build an army, and strike at the very moment things began to feel routine.

30 Days Before Unity

New Alcatraz Prison

The other European inmates held in New Alcatraz clung fast to old party and ethnic lines, segregating themselves to each other's "fellow man." Pavel, tired from being out so many nights, plunked himself down in the mess hall; it was morning.

The same runny, tired eggs. The same dry white toast. The same watered-down orange "drink." "Ham." Pavel kicked his food around on his metal tray with a fork, hardly hungry.

Farther down the table, two Cossacks from the Urals had begun arguing. It turns out, back in Russia, the man yelling had his daughter and several animals stolen by the fat, guilty looking, fellow. The yelling man made public the knowledge that the accused had used the stolen daughter as a *seamstress* and the pigs as *lovers*.

Pavel, tired of this useless infighting, stood and threw his tray at the man yelling. The eggs smacked the fellow in his face, then slid eagerly to the floor.

"You! You are going to replace my pigs!?"

"To hell with your pigs! To hell with you! And you!" Pavel pointed at both men. "Why are we fighting *each other?* We are all fellows, kidnapped prisoners, are we not? What you are mad about happened *years* ago! Time to move on!"

"Move on to what?" The yelling man postured, looking around with his arms spread wide open.

"Shut it up, or we'll shit you up!" A guard snarled at the quarreling men.

Pavel shook his head and left the mess hall to hit the showers. On his way to wash off the lingering effects of proto-tribal-nationalism, an announcement blared over the ancient loudspeaker system.

Crsshh Today, there will be a special news broadcast at 1400pm, mandatory for all inmates, that is all… *Crsshh* The message repeated in Russian, Bulgarian, Ukrainian, and several other central Asian languages.

Pavel looked at one of the many, many, analog clocks that grew like mold throughout the prison island. It was 1300pm.

The inmates of New Alcatraz, false beards and all, were gathered into the island's multi-purpose room. There were old, wooden, folding chairs arranged into rows and columns.

"Find a seat, sit down, and shut up!" Another nameless guard howled at the European prisoners. Imported prison guards repeated the command in their respective languages.

A screen rolled down from the ceiling and a projector clicked on.

"Lights out!"

"Good evening, this is Maurice Breadsalt with the evening news…"

No date was given.

"The on-going race war that originally erupted in the Mid-West has spread across the country. Police are stretched thin, and the National Guard has been called in to places like Detroit, Tulsa, Milwaukee, Oakland, and Seattle, just to name a few…" Everything that was said was also displayed on the bottom of the screen in Russian subtitles only.

"The war started after several unkind remarks from the famous Florida Oligarch Ted Gotsis made their way onto Social Media. Mr. Gotsis very publicly shamed and fired his maids, who were African-American and Latino, after what he alleges was a failed sexual extortion plot.

"The maids have since denied any wrongdoing, but his insistence on the Latina's deportation and the imprisonment of the African-American has lit a match in the tinderbox of American race relations."

There was footage of rioting, police cars, people screaming. None of it dated, all of it varying in quality from 4K HD to old VHS tapes.

"The President has sued for peace, but to no avail…"

The newscaster droned on. There were interviews with affected people. Some of them looked oddly familiar to Pavel.

I swear she's a nurse in the Sick Bay… Pavel thought as he carefully took in the newscast.

"… In other news, Shiva, the disease and not the Hindu deity, continues to spread. A new directive from President De La Croix mandates inoculations for all incarcerated individuals across the country…"

Inoculations? Pavel thought.

When it was over, the inmates were directed back to their cells. On his way back, Pavel recognized an old, dear, friend.

"Lachlan!"

"Pavel?"

The two broke off from the rest and hid in the Library.

"My god, how did they get you?" Pavel asked Lachlan.

"I was doing time in Graz for credit card fraud when I was drugged. I next woke with this damned beard stuck to my flesh and more police than I had ever seen. I was in someplace called 'New Orlee-anns' and I was being arrested for threatening a doctor in the name of fucking Islamic Charles Darwin! What about you?"

"I was home! In Budapest! I go to sleep one night, I wake up robbing a Hooters in Nashville, Tennessee the next… also in the name of Charles Darwin!"

"Somebody is pissed about that serial number they found on human DNA!"

"I used to be an atheist before they found that, too," Pavel spoke softly to his friend. "I understand why someone would be upset, but an entire elaborate charade? And for what? Why are we here? Why all these new Japanese medical staff? What is in the injections they're going to give us?"

"Shhh, calm down my friend. Here, take this."

"What is it?"

"One of those sexy little nurses in Sick Bay, she gave this to me. She says it is berry full of rohypnol!"

"Why would I want this?"

"I don't know. She has several *bottles* of them and gave me one in case I can't sleep, her words."

"Do you have insomnia?" Pavel still couldn't understand why he was being offered the piece of fruit.

"You don't?" Lachlan was averaging around four hours of sleep a night. He had been on Alcatraz for a week. "Do you know where we are?"

"…Yes. Do you?"

"…No…"

"C'mon Lachlan! I thought you were old FSB, eh?"

"Shhh, Pavel!"

"We're in San Francisco. On that island prison that was so famous."

"Alcatraz?"

"Da."

"Shit. From Graz to San Francisco, huh?"

"So it would seem…"

"Well, take the berry anyways. You never know when it may come in handy," Lachlan the Hungarian-Russian former FSB man winked at his old friend Pavel. "And, because you told *me* where we are in the world, I'll tell *you* a little something: The news we just watched was entirely fake! A PsyOp! The newscaster and I did several missions together for the UN's Intelligence division. All the footage was either staged or from things in no way related to what was reported."

"That's why the quality of the footage varied so greatly!"

"Da, indeed."

"But, Lachlan, why?"

"Oh, my friend, that is the answer I, too, seek. Take the berry."

"Ok ok, I'll take it."

A noise from nearby, someone had entered the library.

"Better hurry back before they catch us and beat us!" Pavel said.

The two men hugged and went their separate ways, back to their cells.

Pavel and the rest of the inmates let the news broadcast sink in. With what Lachlan said about all of it being a lie, Pavel still wondered why it was shown in the first place. Every man here came from somewhere in Europe. Why should they care about violent racism in America? Lachlan did say it was most likely a PsyOp; but why, and to what end? Whatever the reason, the desired effect from rampant chaos occurring on the outside was palpable on the inside of Alcatraz, especially amongst those whose mental faculties were not their strong suit.

16 Days Before Unity

New Alcatraz Prison

Pavel was retiring to his cell after a long night out exploring the island. He had started to notice the other inmates behaving strangely after the "inoculations" had began. Pavel had yet to receive his. At first he thought maybe it had something to do with the purported race war happening just beyond the frigid waters of the San Francisco Bay. However, his old friend, Lachlan of the FSB, consistently reminded him that the war they were all constantly told was raging on, in fact, simply wasn't.

"An unexpected anathema" had disrupted the supply line of anticipated medicine and doctors coming from Japan. The TASC staff already on Alcatraz Island had to create Amplified Reality on the fly, as their superiors were no longer answering their phones. Emails went unread. Given the implications of their work, and the Non-Disclosure Agreements they had all signed, the TASC staff resolved to simply do their best and to carry the original plans as intended, barring any updates. So far, the inmates were behaving like inmates: up at 0600am, fed by 0800am, recreation until 1200pm, lunch at 1230pm, afternoon tasks completed by 1600pm, dinner at 1730pm, back in cells by 1900pm, lights out at 2000pm. This mechanical existence could certainly continue, but the Amplified Reality would run out, eventually.

Pavel's cell faced the northeast, looking towards Albany and with the old Alcatraz tourist dock just in view. Every night at 0245am, two uniformed men would walk down to the tourist dock and into a new-looking Quonset hut that stretched across the docks. In the mornings, this dock was primarily used for any shipments to the island. The island was at 80% self-sufficiency but still needed a few toiletries and maintenance items brought in from time to time. Being an electrical engineer, he also noticed the apparatus extending from the hut. His eyes followed the thick bundle of wiring from the hut, until they disappeared into the guardhouse at the foot of the facility. *Something is not right*, he thought to himself. The big tip off indicating something strange was the steam emanating from the water around the dock.

A few nights later when he had a better opportunity, Pavel took a deep breath and once more slid out into the night. He slithered from bush to bush, stalking his uniformed prey, a Japanese named Toshi. Toshi was careless his entire life, and tonight would prove to be another addition to his personal journal of aloofness; he carried a little yellow book of his personal indiscretions in his front right pocket at all times.

At 0305am Toshi and Daineko left the hut and went their separate ways to their respective living quarters. Toshi hummed the theme to an old anime about samurai robot cats running a pizza parlor and overlooked the tripwire. Toshi ate the ground with gusto and laid there, face down, for a time, deciding how this entry would unfold in his journal. Before he could settle on a font, Pavel was upon him. Pavel received his training during the wars needed to create the New Austria-Hungary in Budapest. His specialty was kidnappings and interrogation. At the time, the Hungarian government believed the Serbian Muslims were coordinating bombings with the Earth Liberation Front in an attempt to force the Hungarians into neo-veganism, the current threat of choice for the world at-large. Pavel was trained and deployed to extract information from traveling imams, and he was very, very good at his job.

Pavel gagged Toshi with a sock and took him into a large bush that concealed a hollow perfect for hiding bodies. Here he made use of the discarded hemp stalks that now littered the island and bound him. Toshi's uniform was snug on Pavel, but did it the trick.

Pavel scampered back to the Quonset hut, but the door was locked. *Right*, he thought to himself, *the keycard.* With one swipe he was in.

Pavel shut the door gently behind him and crept forward. The hut and its contents were not to be found anywhere on all the wall-mounted diagrams he had spied during his nights out. True, the *dock* was on all of the island diagrams, but the *hut* itself was an anomaly. It was *very* warm and *very* humid inside the hut. Pavel began sweating as he crept around from box to box. Above him, he saw a small room, suspended from the ceiling by cables on a series of tracks. It appeared the room could move to any part of the large hut and raise or lower itself as well, at least according to the pulleys he saw. The room had windows on all sides and he could make out two or three figures in the room, sitting with their backs to him. Two of the figures were smoking curly, elaborate looking pipes. The kinds of pipes one would use to enjoy Amplified opium. The kind of opium that didn't cause you to black out for hours, but instead gave you the euphoric universal acceptance all opium products do, but with enough insomniex woven into its genetic fabric that you were actually more alert after smoking it. The third figure was wearing the newest issue of the SF Chronicle on his face. He was casually viewing the digital pages through his glasses.

Pavel crept out just enough to see beneath the crow's nest and saw exactly what was turning the Quonset hut into a hot and steamy swamp; a Trident D-5 class nuclear submarine. The hatch was open and out of it came a mass of wires and cables that lead to a transformer at the opposite end of the hut. "Боже мой" he said out loud.

Pavel was in disbelief. *The foolishness! The folly! The short-sightedness of it all! Why?* He thought, *why would you use a nuclear submarine to power this facility? Doesn't the grid provide enough power? Why not solar power?*

There was movement in the crow's nest. The whole apparatus came to life and began to glide towards the transformer. Once overhead, an emissary dropped down next to the giant electrical box via a rope ladder. He began tweaking and prodding and eventually the other two stuck their heads out to watch. *Now*, Pavel thought. He climbed to his feet, ran, and dove onto the D-5 Sub. He scurried along the surface and dove into the hatch, landing on his upper back on top of the bundle of wires. The men at the transformer didn't flinch. Pavel was in.

Pavel stood up and rubbed in between his shoulder blades. He began exploring the vessel, meticulously looking here and there, consuming information about this now retired maritime siege engine. He tested out the bunks, drank some of the water from the desalinization spout and made his way to the weapons gallery. The whole place was stripped bare. No bullets, no knives, not even pictures of torpedoes, nothing.

Pavel felt a sudden, overwhelming sense of defeat. The resentment he'd built towards the capitalists who brought him here couldn't manifest itself into anything vengeful, given the circumstances. Pavel shook his head, gave several tuts to no one, and decided to pack it in for the night. As he made his way to the hatch, he saw something glimmer in the red light of the submarine's interior. He peered through a mass of wiring and welding and spotted the corner of a warning label. He reached in and pushed aside some of the sloppy engineering work and found something that exceeded his wildest dreams. The lettering on the circular device read 'W-76 100kt.' He'd seen this before, at the institute where he was given his engineering degree.

This was a warhead.

A 100-kiloton warhead to be exact.

"Yeah we left an old Dubya-76 on board in case of an emergency, y'know, something goes wrong, the prisoners revolt, develop super powers, etc. we have no idea what TASC and those Japanese are really up to. Hell, if they can make flowers that release narcotics, I don't even want to know what they're putting into the blood of those *deviants*." Mansfield 'Butch' Cairns was busy reassuring president De La Croix via holophone that everything at New Alcatraz was going fine. "Oh don't worry Pick, we've hid it in the one place not even the workers can get to... Uh huh..."

Pavel stopped daydreaming and took stock of the setup. The TASC engineers had rigged the subs reactor to power the island via the transformer. The cooling is being handled by the frigid waters of the bay, and he noticed that if the core temperature began to climb, the submarine could flood itself and continue supplying power. It was sweltering in the steel tube. If his plan was going to happen, he'd better do it soon. He found a notepad and pen that had been left behind and made a quick wiring diagram of what he saw. He listened for the crow's nest, but they were still occupied. He crept up the ladder, caught a glimpse of all three men now out of the crow's nest, inspecting the transformer, and hopped out. When it was clear, he hid under an overturned box and quietly slithered out of the Quonset hut.

He bolted for the bush and found that Toshi was still there, out cold. Pavel redressed him and stuffed the rohypnol-berry from Lachlan into Toshi's mouth. He massaged his throat until the little fruit was gone and then dragged his limp body towards the hut. Pavel dropped Toshi's arms, apologized in Russian, and took off for his cell. It was 0430am and the guards were getting set to change shift.

Safely in his rotting cell, Pavel feigned sleep but could barely contain himself. Jittery, his legs danced like he was a boy again. It took all his will to keep them steady as the new guards now roamed his wing, checking on every inmate.

Morning slapped Pavel awake. His meager two-and-a-half hours of sleep weighed on his forehead. His "beard" itched. The bars on his entrance slid back. It was time for the morning shower. In the hot steam, Pavel eyed another man. Pavel had been feeling out the other inmates, seeking trust beyond the ever-busy Lachlan. One man, in spite of his false Darwinian beard also being semi-permanent, did stand out, Pyotr Ivanovich.

Pyotr was from Lviv and had ties to cells in Serbia. He told Pavel that he was arrested for plotting an attack on the Verkovna Rada as retribution for ignoring his villages multiple requests for protection from the roving Scottish hoards now-so-prominent in that region. Pyotr was shrewd, spoke little, and, most importantly, was full of anger. He was short, but stout, and bore a prominent birthmark on his neck. On his left hand were Eastern Coded Tattoos, indicating his faction, tribe, and level of loyalty.

The two men exchanged nods of understanding and prepared to greet each other. After the shower, they casually began their conversation in the library. While feeling each other out as comrades, each man was able to determine that the other was competent enough to engage in conversation in an obscure dialect. Pavel initially chose to do this in order to keep others ignorant of his findings. Once Pavel had secured Pyotr as a trusted ally, Pavel told Pyotr about the sub, and it's forgotten warhead.

"No!"

"Yes! I would not believe had I not found it!"

"Hmm, so what we do with this information?"

"Well, I know enough to get things into place, and I am able to access the sub at night. The only problem, I cannot activate the warhead, as this is the limit of my studies."

"I see, I spent time in the Ukrainian navy before I began to loathe Kiev. If I could have serial number from device, I may recall how to arm it."

"Ok, I will make expedition tonight to retrieve number. Let us talk again tomorrow, at lunch."

Night fell like a soft blanket onto New Alcatraz. The whole island served as a quiet witness to the stillness of the night. Pavel, feeling the weight of the moonlight, stealthily crept amongst the shrubs and topiaries leading up to the Quonset hut that housed the sub. This time, the guards were huddled around an outdoor three-dimensional projection of the Nagoya Basho Sumo tournament emanating from the Restored Empire of Japan. Pavel was feeling cavalier, so he slipped over to the door, and using the keycard he kept, he was in.

The mobile crow's nest was also lit up by the Nagoya Basho, Pavel let out a sigh of relief. Once inside the sub, he located the warhead and, using a sharpie he stole from a nurse, he wrote the serial number on his arm.

He poked his head out and noticed the crow's nest now directly over the entrance to the sub. Sweat began leaking from his pores, causing him annoyance. *Do I wait*, Pavel asked himself, *or do I risk getting forgotten in the isolation gulag?* Suddenly, chatter. Pavel could make out the Japanese guards emphatically reacting to several matches from the Nagoya Basho. As their steps got closer, Pavel grew more weary. The sound of a boot on the hull made Pavel scamper underneath a piloting console. Holding his breath, Pavel began shaking as he watched the slow march of boots descending into the sub.

The Japanese had begun their nightly inspection of the reactor and the sub itself. The first guard, tall and skinny Masato Tanaka, picked up the clipboard from its wall hook and commenced checking off items as he went. The second guard, the left-handed and athletic Kiyoji Mushiba, stood restlessly near the ladder. Kiyoji had money riding on a few Ozeki and Yokuzuna level bouts, and his fighters were kyujo just the day before. Tonight, though, they had showed up to fight, but as for how ready their bodies were, Kiyoji had his doubts.

Masato took his time, having already lost money to his boss and brother-in-law, Kiyoji, on a questionable uwatenage by a controversial fighter, Takanoyama II. Masato tapped the pen on his clipboard, now stalling on purpose just to get at Kiyoji. The time for sanyaku bouts was fast approaching, and Masato wanted his coworker to be uneasy. Pavel, getting worse by the minute, suppressed his colon's natural desire to groan when under stress as best he could. It did not prove to be enough, though, as his quivering intestines rumbled and squeaked while trying to contain himself.

"Did you hear that?" Masato called to Kiyoji.

"What?" Kiyoji was deep in thought, hands shoved deep in his pockets. He was feverishly working out how to explain the large financial losses to his wife. Couple that with his itching need to get out of the hot and cramped metal tube as soon as he could, and you get a dazed and drifting Kiyoji: on the job but mentally checked out.

Masato, being married to Kiyoji's sister Kumiko, had nothing to explain to her. His conscience was clean.

"I heard a sound, like a hungry belly or something rumbling…" For some reason, Masato squinted in order to hear better.

"Look, I'm done." Kiyoji was getting agitated by his coworker's actions. "Also, you forget we are inside a *very old* submarine. This rust-tube creaks and moans all the time. C'mon, time for *you* to lose to *me*."

"Hmm, no. I heard a noise."

"No?! You tell me no?! Get back up that ladder before I tell my sister what you look at while we're on the clock!"

"Psh, some brother-in-law you are. Worthless."

Masasto finished his delay and hung the clipboard back on its hook. The two hustled quickly back up the ladder and into the crow's nest. The structure then smoothly glided back to the opposite end of the Quonset hut and was once more relit by the Sumo taking place in the Empire of Japan.

Pavel felt his heart in his throat. He rolled out from under the console and crept back up the ladder. Cautiously he made his way out of the sub and towards the entrance. The door slid shut and Pavel, no longer feeling all that cavalier, bolted back to his cell.

Back inside, Pavel could barely catch his breath. His heart pounded and the walls of his cell were panting along with him. His hands shook. His false beard was almost suffocating. The glue keeping the Darwinian fallacy attached to him showed no signs of weakening. He checked his arm for the serial and noticed a deft smudge.

He glared at the damaged writ on his arm, begging his mind to remember what it was. *Is that a 4? An A? What did I write!? Those guards,* he thought, *that's why it got smudged.* Before cursing and falling asleep, Pavel resolved the digit to be a 4.

The following morning, Pavel gave a sign to Pyotr and the meeting was confirmed. At lunch, the two men poured over a plan.

"...the last digit is 4."

"You are sure of this?"

"Yes."

"Ok, because there were several of this model and the wiring is specific for each. I use my library time to map schematic and will smuggle to you via sock."

"Ok great... Then what?"

The two men looked at each other. Neither had thought to ask that. Hostages? Ransom? Escape? Pavel just wanted to go home. Pyotr longed to bring down the oppressive regime that extradited him to America. Both men lacked a true criminals mind. They had the tools and the will and the ability, just not the know-how.

"This is good question. 'Then What?' Perhaps we need a third?" Pyotr suggested.

"Hmm, that could work. But whom?" Pavel of course thought of Lachlan, but he had not seen him anywhere on the island after their initial run-in.

"I will point him out in showers tomorrow. He is very rough man. Many crimes. You meet him and casually chat, tell him our findings. He will tell us what to do."

The White House

The laughter emanating from the Carter Solarium trickled through the out-turned transom above the entrance. Diamond De La Croix prided herself on her infectious cachinnating. Another thing she was proud of was the 'arrangement' she was able to manipulate her husband into; that of being able to freely spend as much time as she wished with a prominent member of Pickford's cabinet.

A trio of maids floated by the glass and wrought iron construct that allowed one entry into the lush greenhouse. President Pickford-Saxby De La Croix, a Dixiecrat from Louisiana, studied the cute and demure women in black and white as they scurried about. The heavy breathing and occasional chortle from the solarium slid right off his back.

Although not entirely sure of why he tortured himself like this, he was sure that he absolutely had to allow it to continue.

Pickford-Saxby checked his binary watch, a gift from the Japanese Consulate, and let out a gruff sigh, allowing his lips to flap.

At long last, the noises stopped, and the pair emerged from their den.

First out was Mansfield 'Butch' Cairns. The tall, flat-faced man with no upper lip adjusted his tie and failed to notice the President standing in a nearby alcove.

Mansfield ran a whale's bone comb through his hair and lifted the face of his watch to reveal a secret compartment containing a shimmering white powder. The man licked the tip of his right pinky and collected a smattering of the powder which he then rubbed into his nostrils. An aide appeared and began going over several items on a tablet as the two walked away.

After another couple of minutes, the First Lady emerged from her floral escape and motioned to begin her trek to the oval office when she was interrupted.

"We're late."

"Oh! You startled me," Diamond De La Croix clutched at her chest in alarm. "How long have you been there?"

"Long enough," the President regarded his 'wife' with impatience.

"Look, Pick, we talked about this-"

"I know, I know. I'll stop doing this to myself eventually… It is for the 'Republic' after all… But could you at least *bathe* every now and again?"

"Indeed, it is for the Republic, and he *likes* me unwashed… And just what are we late for now?"

"Tea with Rutherford Yun-Ping. We'll be discussing his latest plans to ensure the safety of all UN-member-heads-of-state."

"Oh?"

"Yeah, it's some radical new idea… getting a lot of buzz from several so-called 'presidents for life,'" the American President said, leading his wife down the hallway lined with portraits.

"Who else will be there?"

"Butch, Charles, Philippe, Meinhardt, Gao, and Toshiro."

"...Really?" the FLOTUS stopped in her tracks. "Where's all the security?"

"Diamond, this meeting was flagged as Non-Hostile," the President informed his partner while grabbing her by the upper arm. "The fact that *you're* being allowed in is something I'll have to take up with Butch. When we get in there, not a word from you."

The two ambled into the Trump Solarium on the other side of the White House and claimed their seats at the immense wooden table. All around them, and the other heads of state, were alien-looking plants. The purpose of the dense foliage was dual: the plants therein were all brand new, pre-production, hybridized narcotic creations and were therefore on display, in addition to serving as privacy shields.

Hellos and greetings were exchanged, then the man himself strode in.

"Hello, hello and welcome to this meticulously scheduled meeting," Rutherford Yun-Ping's oily smooth baritone voice gave all in attendance an uneasy calm. President Pickford then noticed several strange things about the Secretary General. There was a light dew on his brow. His cheeks were flush. His fingernails were corroded and spotty. A certain musk reminiscent of a medical school hung around him.

As the Secretary General sauntered around the glass construct, he made sure that he touched every single person, something the PM of Japan did not take too kindly to. When he did, his hands left a light dusting on the shoulders of whomever he touched, similar to dandruff.

"Rutherford! What is the meaning of this!" Toshiro Agabusa called out.

Rutherford smiled and exposed a set of rotten teeth. He then tittered, giggled, and lunged at the PM's throat, fetid claws extended.

With near instantaneous speed, the PM's guard produced a tanto sword which was then deftly plunged into Rutherford's midsection with a samurai war whoop.

Rutherford stumbled back, clutching his stomach, when he once more dove for the Japanese Prime Minister. This time, the guard produced a luger pistol and fired a shot into the left temple of Rutherford Yun-Ping.

The force of the bullet wrenched half of his face off.

Mrs. De La Croix was the first to notice the unnaturalness of the scene before the group.

There was no blood.

Instead, a thick green unction took its place.

The body then stumbled backward while convulsing and collapsed into its assigned chair. The corpse twitched and spurted green ooze for several minutes thereafter.

Diamond, her mouth agape in horror, rose from her own comfortable chair and moved to turn around the swivel seat containing the now-dead UN Secretary General.

On the inside of his coat, Diamond noticed a flower she had never seen before. It was a parasitic Cuscuta plant and it was leeching from a quaint little daisy.

"Don't touch that! Don't smell it, don't do anything!" Butch Cairns was standing now, eager to protect his fragrant woman.

"Oh my…"

"Fred," President Pickford-Saxby spoke into his collar-mounted communication device. "We need a clean up crew in the Trump Solarium. We've got some kind of unauthorized narcoplant in here and a dead Secretary General to go with it…"

After the body was removed and the flower sent to the in-house lab, it was discovered that the parasitic Cuscuta had grafted into Rutherford Yun-Ping's central nervous system. The daisy was hybridized to include something TASC synthesized called 'rage-itol'; originally meant for soldiers in the heat of battle, this was a substance that induced fierce anger, avarice, and intense hallucinations as a side-effect. Typically, this drug required a medium of an animal derivative, usually gelatin, to become potent and effective. Seeing this compound present in a parasitic flower, though, was a new, horrifying, discovery.

Together with the Cuscuta, Rutherford Yun-Ping's mind was not even close to his own.

"Whoever did this knew what they're doing when it came to plant hybridization…" The British Prime Minister said.

"Do you think TASC is behind this?" President Pickford-Saxby may have been an addict, a coward, and a money-grubbing sonofabitch, but he was no idiot.

"What? No! They just transferred several billion dollars into the Federal Reserve. Why pay us to test their drugs on our people, and then kill a diplomat in the White House? No way…" Butch Cairns facetious comforting concealed the fact that knew the truth. He knew with all certainty that if the White House physio-botanists were able to check the molecular structure of the Cuscuta alone, they would most certainly find Kenji Hirasawa's trademarked molecular bonding.

New Alcatraz Prison

The following morning, in the showers, Pyotr used an unkempt toenail to indicate to Pavel who would be their third. A Chechen, the man's body bore the markings of one who had spent time in the Russian correctional system; the spires on his back serving as an indication of whereabouts he had spent that time and why.

At lunch, the three men sat down and began their congress.

"Pavel, this is Alyosha. Alyosha, Pavel."

The two men skittishly shook hands and resumed guardedly eating their ersatz breakfast. Today's meal was 'grapefruit' and 'brown sugar' with 'sausages' and orange drink.

Clearing his throat, Alyosha removed bits of 'grapefruit' from his red, fake, beard and eyed Pavel.

"Pyotr tells me you have access to W-76 Trident D5 warhead?" He smirked, "Hmph, this is fantasy." Shaking his head, Alyosha methodically chewed his 'sausage' with a sturdy confidence.

"Fantasy? No, this is the truth. I-" Pavel stopped himself as he felt it best not to reveal himself. Pavel didn't know Alyosha, who was already suspicious of Pavel himself. "I promise, I have access to said device."

"Hm, I do not believe you."

"Pyotr, find someone else. Someone who isn't this

ignorant." Pavel clicked his teeth and shoved a forkful of 'food' into his mouth.

Alyosha jumped to a stand and his eyes blazed.

"Ignorant!? If we were in Chechnya, I-"

"You'd what?" Pavel rose and matched the red-bearded hulk's energy. "I was kidnapped from my home. I had a false beard plastered onto my face and was forced to be arrested for nothing! Now I am here, and I don't even know where *here* is! Now sit down and eat your breakfast *like a good dog!*" Pavel stood firm, having barked his agitation at Alyosha. He chose to feign ignorance as to their mutual location in the San Francisco Bay. Pavel learned at an early age that one must never show their whole hand. Alyosha was stunned, yet he concealed it, of course. Slowly sitting back down, Alyosha took a swig of the orange drink and swallowed hard.

"Where is this device?" Alyosha said without making eye contact.

"This is for me to know right now. Just…" Pavel hesitated. The thought, the realization of what they were doing stormed its way into his frontal lobe. *Am I really asking how to be a criminal?* He thought. *No wonder this man doesn't believe us! Who asks how to commit atrocities?* Steadying himself, Pavel gathered his thoughts. "Alyosha, we have a nuke. Simple. We want out of this illegal facility, wherever the hell we are. Simple. We have come to you, no, decided to include you in our plans, because Pyotr says you can devise the best possible use of my discovery. Simple. Tell me, are you content here? Do you want to stay? Huh? *Like a good dog?*"

Alyosha jumped at the dog remark. After a pause,

"Ok. I will craft something. How soon can the device be armed?"

"Pyotr?"

"Yes, I have made the arming schematic but, not here. I will bring to you when we pass each other during the library exchange."

"Ok, once I have the schematic, I will wait for something from you, Alyosha, then I will head to the device and arm it."

"How soon should I move?" Alyosha, now resolute and focused gazed fixedly at Pavel.

"We move in 2 weeks time."

12 Hours Before Unity

New Alcatraz Prison

The day was here.

Over the previous fortnight, Alyosha had begun consolidating who he was able to really trust in his circle for the plan he and his other two cohorts had devised. In the mess hall, the men would meet in the mornings and speak in their unique and clunky dialect to avoid detection. The plan grew legs, then arms and finally a head cropped up.

"Hostages?"

"Yes! It is perfect!"

"First, Pyotr, you will feign injury or illness and get taken to the sick bay. Here, my cousin Vasily will make a scene, causing the guards to rush in. Your arrival, Pyotr, will be his signal. Now, I've made nice with the nurse that gives me my so-called 'vitamin shots.' I will get her to let me into the joint supply closet," he winked. "Then I will knock her out and use her keycard to open the other door in the joint closet and tear into the fracas Vasily has started. Armed with medical waste, I will jab a few guards with dirty needles to show we're serious and take the rest hostage."

"How will I be signaled?" Pavel hung on every word.

"Hm, I guess I will have to shove something out of the window to signal you, wherever you'll be." Alyosha gave a look of contempt to Pavel, as he had still not revealed the exact location of the warhead.

"This plan, it sounds like it could work." Pyotr was near giddy with excitement.

"It *will* work," Alyosha spoke with absolute seriousness. "Everything is in place. You two came to the right fellow to organize your mal-intentions. Once you have been to as many prisons as I have, you begin to see that all are not so different." Alyosha finished. Pavel, in response, concluded his 'breakfast' and left the table. "I'm going to lift some weights and burn off this adrenaline." Turning back, he mouthed *tonight* to Pyotr and Alyosha as he rounded the corner.

1 Hour Before Unity

As the sun set, Pavel sat nervously in his cell. *This is it!* He thought. *No going back!* He rocked on the edge of his cot, tapping his shoes on the cold concrete.

A creaking, wobbly wheel broke his introverted trance. A gurney wheeled past his cell. On it was Pyotr, shaking and clutching at his stomach, foam appeared at the edges of his mouth. Pavel leapt and took out his hand mirror and used it to visually follow Pyotr down the gangway. *Something's not right,* he thought. *Pyotr looked a little too convincing.*

The sun had now set, Pavel's cue. He scampered the eight feet across his cell and dislodged the same familiar bricks. Seeing Pyotr convulsing on that gurney wouldn't leave. *Pyotr looked like he was crying for help!* Pavel's stomach turned but he knew to press on. Being trapped here and experimented on was worse than all seven levels of hell.

Taking his usual path, Pavel at last came upon the door to his destiny.

Toshi was back on duty, a boon for Pavel. Toshi was promptly pulled into the same sagebrush and was unconscious in seconds. Pavel again swapped clothing and collected the much needed keycard.

Pavel swiped, the door opened, he was in.

He craned his neck to peer into the Quonset hut, spying out the crow's nest.

The mobile observation cube rested at the rear of the sub again. The two Japanese guards were asleep. This puzzled Pavel as it was only 2130pm. Regardless, he pressed on.

Pavel crept over to the hatch and cop-rolled down into the old sub.

He nearly slipped as he slid down the ladder. Sweat was pouring down his face and arms. He scrambled over to where he had hid the device. There it sat. Thirty-six inches of nuclear freedom.

Taking the schematic from his sock, he cursed. His nervous sweating had caused some of the schematic to be slightly illegible. *Damn cheap prison pens,* he thought. Working to calm himself, Pavel took a deep breath and began trying to decipher and implement the now blotchy schematic.

Alyosha watched the sunset with focus. His mind concentrated on his role in this plan and how he hadn't been completely honest with Pavel and Pyotr. Alyosha always ran solo, a fact he purposefully neglected to impart to the others.

After Pavel had left to work-out earlier, Alyosha added some pills he'd been hoarding into Pyotr's drink and made him swallow the whole thing.

Several hours later, the effect from the pills had begun peaking. This created a genuine-enough emergency for the guards to come and do their best ambulance impression.

As the gurney squeaked by Alyosha's cell, he used the phone smuggled into him via the Japanese nurse to alert her. Not ten minutes later were there two more guards outside Alyosha's cell ready to take him to the sick bay for an impromptu evaluation of the effects of his specific pill regimen.

Once out of detectable range, Alyosha and Yuki made love in the joint supply closet. Not long after, the pills reached their zenith, and Pyotr began convulsing.

Alyosha swiped the card from Yuki's waist, shoved her to the ground, and sprang from the joint closet. He immediately lunged for the red sharps box on the wall and spun around with a handful of needles. Guards came at him from all sides but the crusted syringes in his hands kept them at more than arm's length.

One guard activated his stun-baton and dove at

Alyosha. With an unusual smoothness Alyosha side stepped him and buried a needle into his neck, depressing the plunger. The man gasped and writhed on the floor. The filthy air bubble had been injected directly into his carotid. Within seconds, the man grabbed his head and began shrieking. In the confusion, Alyosha bounded off of other gurneys in a dazzling display of agility. One-by-one the guards fell, each with his own needle, fatally lodged somewhere in their bodies.

A nurse jumped for and hit the alarm. TASC never finished properly setting up the facility on Alcatraz Island, so there were no bots to descend from their concealed ceiling posts. The alarm merely lit a red light in the guard's shack, but this was enough to alert them to action.

Alyosha yanked an IV pole out of a patient and bashed one of the security cameras. It fell from its mooring but was saved by its cord. It dangled and spun, giving the people watching it mild motion sickness. Picking it up, Alyosha looked directly into it and began listing his demands.

"Right now, as I speak to you, our leverage is being made ready. If you want to live to see your families again, I suggest you—"

There was a bright flash.

Everything around everyone on Alcatraz Island became humid, Styrofoam, and dull.

There was no noise, nothing to see.

Just white hot emptiness.

An eerie calm forcibly overtook the island, now suddenly devoid of life.

Pavel struggled with the smudged plans, but he did make progress. Each step had to be perfect or, as Pyotr warned him, the warhead could detonate. As time passed, Pavel wondered how Alyosha and Pyotr were fairing on their end. Last he saw Pyotr, he looked a lot worse than he expected. *Was it just good acting?* In the few months they had spent together here he had never got the impression that Pyotr was a good liar. *Was he actually ill? Did Alyosha do something to him to make it more convincing?*

The constant chatter in his mind, the heat from the reactions within the submarine core, how they would manage the hostages, these are the thoughts that occupied Pavel's mind, not the warhead itself.

Without thinking, Pavel had misinterpreted several symbols and had wired the device to go off. The all-hands alarm suddenly came on full blast outside of the submarine. Pavel froze, but didn't hear the crow's nest moving around, nor could he hear the guards scrambling to attention.

Pavel decided to carry on after several tense, but silent, seconds.

Pleased with his 'arming' of the warhead, Pavel crept back up the ladder. He peeked out of the hatch. There was the crow's nest, unmoved from its original spot. The alarm inside was sharply loud, yet the guards remained still; too still. Pavel, always one to feed his curiosity, made his way toward the mechanical nest.

A congealing stream of blood oozed out from

under the door. Pavel worked the door handle with grace. When the door popped open, one of the guards fell out and onto Pavel, pinning him. Pavel wriggled and fought until he was out from under Kiyoji's corpse. When he saw the other guard, Masato, still softly breathing, he climbed up into the nest to see what had killed them.

As he went to examine the half-living Masato, he jolted and convulsed, releasing his last breath. This scared the already on edge Pavel. Recoiling in fear, his hand hit the blood-stained controls, sending the nest speeding towards the other end of the Quonset hut. Desperate, Pavel kept hitting the controls until the nest abruptly stopped over the hatch. The momentum from such rapid movement being brought to a sudden halt jarred the nest loose, causing it to creak and rock forward. Pavel gasped as he watched the mobile office lean, and then tip over, ultimately crashing down onto the submarine hatch.

Inside the submarine, the warhead jostled about. The commotion caused the device to come loose from where Pavel had wedged it, tip over, and land directly onto its incorrectly exposed wiring, thus completing the circuit needed to induce nuclear fission.

In a single frustrated flash of an instant, burning white and grayish nothingness became all that Pavel, Pyotr, Alyosha, Tiburon, Sausalito, and Downtown San Francisco could see.

Ketsu

resolutions

15 July 2115

Unity Day

The Infodrome Newscast at 0800am

"Good morning. We resume our coverage of the immense blast that took place in the 53rd state last night. As many as 3,000 are presumed dead, with at least as many missing. Thankfully, the explosion was centered on Alcatraz Island, reducing the damage area. Here is a graphic demonstrating the radius of the explosion.

"This just in, we're now hearing the explosion was, in fact, *nuclear* in nature… Uh huh, yeah, ok. Sorry folks, I was getting some more details through my earpiece, and there are now reports of a submarine being spotted close to the island in the days prior to the now-nuclear explosion in San Francisco…"

Free Press Alliance Broadcast at 0900am

"Good morning, everyone. Here is a map of the apparent blast radius:

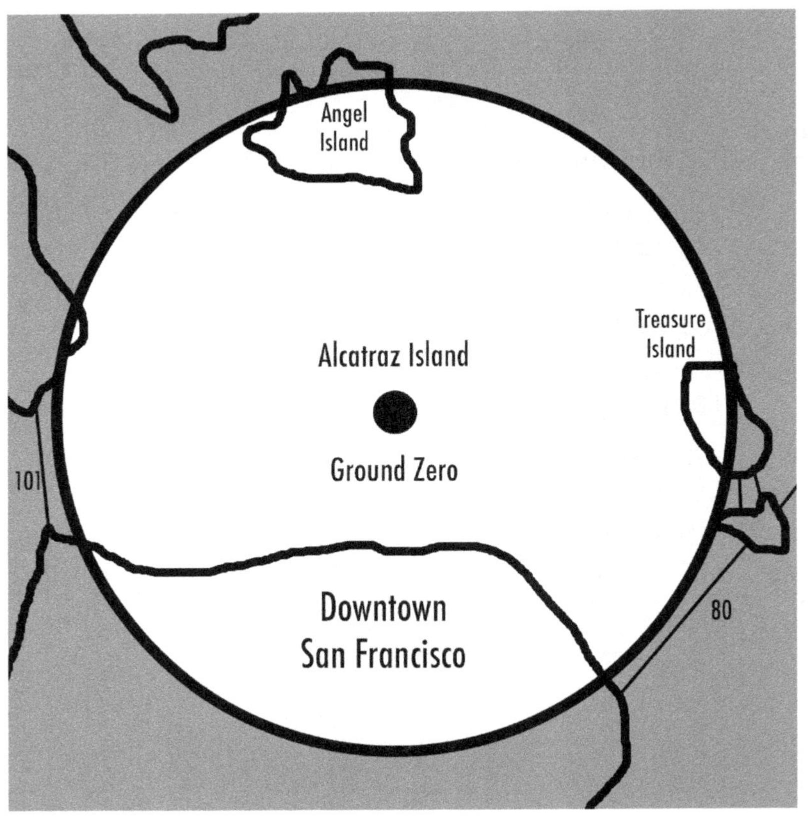

"So far, all life within this white circle has ceased."

NewsNewsNews Broadcast at 1200pm

"Good afternoon. As events continue to unfold following the nuclear blast in San Francisco, details still remain few. The President has issued a statement extending his condolences to those lost, declaring an emergency to allow FEMA to come in and begin clean-up, all while vowing revenge on whoever perpetrated such a heinous act.

"Around the country and around the globe tributes and condolences are pouring in. In the streets of San Francisco, there is anger, confusion, and a heretofore unseen sense of unity and brotherhood amongst locals. The mega-rich of Presidio Heights have opened their homes and kitchens to feed those affected by the sudden loss of life. In the Mission District, restaurants are offering steep discounts.

"Across the Bay, in Oakland, blood banks are at full capacity, yet lines remain winding around city blocks.

"The President had this to say at a press conference held only hours ago:

'Today, we are all hurt. Today we are all sad. Today, we are all San Franciscans…"

Global News Net Broadcast at 1700pm

"The Acting UN Secretary General, a mister Hyrum Jeffs of The United States, serving in the role Rutherford Yun-Ping surrendered upon is sudden, untimely, and unexpected death, has now issued a statement regarding some recent developments out of San Francisco:"

Citizens of the United Nations, this is Acting Secretary General Hyrum Jeffs. A great and concerning incident has occurred within one of our member nations, indeed a permanent member of the Security Council.

In the hours since, it has come to my attention that this act was homegrown. The perpetrators are well known, as is their role in creating the circumstances necessary for the event in question.

Given the already poor handling of the Oil Crisis that is currently crippling our globe, along with the inability to satisfy the will of the people overall, the UN is invoking Article 939. Effective starting at Midnight tonight.

All UN Ambassadors and affiliates are hereby instructed to break the metal seal on the blue boxes you were all given upon your swearing in. Follow the instructions *closely*.

Brothers, Sisters, Citizens of Earth: The United Nations is here to protect you. The United Nations is here to serve you. Please, do not resist.

The White House at 2200pm

"Butch? Butch!?"

"Yes, Mr. President?"

"Butch, where are my LoRoses?"

"Here, sir. Have you fasted?"

"Of course I have! Sorry for yelling..." The President took a long, deep, drag on a bulbous LoRose.

"It's all right. The pod is down this stairwell," Butch Cairns led the President down a very old brick stairwell that led beneath 1600 Pennsylvania Avenue.

"Here we are, sir."

"Oh God... Oh GOD! Article 939... That damn *letter*... Who the hell does the UN think they are!? They can't just *dissolve* the US of A!"

Article 939, as stipulated by the Security Council, effectively dissolves the corporation known as the United States, created in 1928 and backed by the League of Nations. After the bombs were dropped in WW2, the other nations of the global entity met in secret to assure their future, no matter who was elected to lead the "Free World". The Article called upon Mexico and Canada to shut their borders immediately and to subsequently line them with military units. The UN had sleeper agents in key positions of the Federal Government just in case the order needed to be executed.

Governors, Senators, Judges, Sheriffs, County Chairs, and Mayors across the country were suddenly, instantly turned on by their aides and given the directive to 'Comply or Die!'

Most, if not all, died.

The offices of those who chose death were filled by the person who did the killing, loyal to the UN, of course. The Article also outlined the means by which great cities like New York, Chicago, Dallas, Los Angeles, Seattle, and others could convert into Nation States that were effectively vassals for various high-ranking UN proles.

As the President and his VEEP panicked their way to escape, Washington DC was burning and slowly being flooded by elite UN Soldiers.

"I know, I know," Butch Cairns comforted the hyperventilating President De La Croix.

"Why, why is it so *small?*"

"That's because it was meant just for you."

"What about Diamond?"

"She's on her way," Butch Cairns lied.

Diamond De La Croix had fled the country with her beau, Senator Chisholm (I – San Francisco) in the cacophony immediately following the blast. Chisholm had vanished for a time to handle some business directly related to New Alcatraz, but had since returned and taken Diamond before the blast in San Francisco.

"Good, good, I need to see her face before I'm frozen… How long will the battery last?"

"I'm told at least a thousand years, Mr. President."

"*A thousand?* Oh god, oh GOD!"

"Sir, please, take another drag and try to relax. You need to be calm before we can freeze you."

"The walls, tell me about the walls," President De La Croix began chomping on the head of another LoRose.

"The walls here are twenty-two feet thick, all around. The foundation is bolstered into the bedrock. Once the hatch closes, I can't be opened without a sunstone. Only me, and Diamond have sunstones. You will be protected, the Free World will be protected. Once this all blows over, we'll come and get you, sir."

"Oh God, thank you Butch," The President gasped, finally feeling a morsel of relief.

A blast rocked the White House.

"Butch!"

"Goodnight, sir, see you when this is all over…"

Mansfield 'Butch' Cairns shoved President Pickford De La Croix into the cryonics tube and set the timer on INDEFINITE.

Butch closed the hatch that led into the subterranean chamber and it sealed shut.

Butch then waved his sunstone over the release wheel and marveled at the golden electricity that ensured the President's safety.

Mansfield Cairns then emerged from the staircase and stepped through the hidden doorway and back into the oval office. He turned around and was shot point-blank in the face by a UN Peacekeeper wearing a new uniform. This uniform was armored, impersonal, cyclopean, and robin's egg blue. A word was embossed across the upper back, like a nameplate on a jersey, it read: SOLDAT.

The former Vice President and Secretary of Incarceration's body was collected, cataloged, and buried with full honors.

Within several hours, the White House was then cleared, and scraped from the earth. The building was transported to The Museum of The Former United States of America.

The cryogenic tube holding the last freely-elected President of the United States sat unnoticed, and untouched, buried deep below the empty foundation where the White House once stood.

United Nations Global Headquarters at 0000am

"What's the status of Article 939?" Acting-Secretary General Hyrum Jeffs was in his element on the command deck of UN Headquarters outside New York City.

"Sir, the leadership of the United States has been requisitioned. Congress is unable to convene, the Supreme Court has been liquidated, and the Executive Office is terminated. The Logistics for the Great Abdication are in place." Hamza ibn al-Masri, Jeffs' right-hand, was reading off reports as they came in.

"Good. What about De La Croix?"

"There has been no body recovered, sir."

"But you got Cairns?"

"Yes, sir."

"What about FLOTUS?"

"MIA, sir, along with Senator Chisholm."

"Hm. They'll be dead soon. Is there more?"

"Yes, sir. The individual states are reacting as expected. The Northeast, MidWest, and Pacific states have all sworn fealty, but the South is demanding self-governance."

"Crush them."

"Yes, sir."

"Europe?"

"All on board, save for Russia."

"I'll call them. Asia?"

"Japan, India, and the South East are on board. China is mobilizing their army."

"Gautama Buddha… that's going to be tough. Africa?"

"The Maghreb is ours, all of the Western Sub-Saharan states are largely indifferent, whereas East Africa is onboard, although Kenya is still giving some mild resistance, given the Chinese base on the coast there."

"Hm, give the western states some time, then send ultimatums. The Americas?"

"Canada is on board. Mexico is on board… Just getting word that Central and South America are all also on board."

"Excellent. Right, let's shift troops from Tartaria and surround the Chinese on land. Take the war machine from Congo, and deploy them to-"

"Sir,"

"What?"

"Just getting word that Scotland has declared independence and is moving on… Vietnam."

"*Vietnam?*"

"Yes, sir. Apparently they were missed in our report of the South East, no idea how, and they have sworn fealty to China. Troops are pouring into the North, but the Scotch have already landed on several beaches."

"How?"

"…I'm hearing they used freighters to conceal their troop movements and trains to move heavy equipment.

They've been ready and waiting for this for some time it would appear…"

"Great. Who's commanding the Scottish?"

"Their First Minister, one Angus McDuff, sir."

"Get him on the phone."

"What'd the Scottish have to say, sir?"

"They had cells in Hanoi and Saigon, waiting to strike… there's a leak here, Hamza. McDuff knew *something* and had most of his machinery already in place. He even mentioned something about 'paving the way for things in San Francisco' and a pair of dead Japanese guards…"

"The Scots are notoriously resourceful, sir."

"This is true, but still, something doesn't fit right about their reach and power. Keep an eye on them and make sure they plant *our* flag when Hanoi falls."

"Yes, sir."

"Get Russia on the phone."

"The Russians have agreed to our terms and will work to contain the Chinese. Their idea is to manifest their own take on the Great Wall, isolating China. They're saying their diplomats are keeping the Red Army within the country's borders, for now. We'll need to work fast."

"The troops across Tartaria are repositioning, sir. The Congolese war machine is marching east towards a friendly port in Dar es Salaam; they're crossing Burundi as we speak."

"Excellent. Now let's—" Acting-Secretary General Hyrum Jeffs broke into a violent coughing fit. He brought out his handkerchief and brought it to his lips. There was blood, and not a just a little bit.

"Are you ok, sir?"

"Yes, yes, I'm fine," Hyrum Jeffs answered in a dry rasp before being taken again into a hacking fit. His eyes bulged and he stumbled into a chair.

"Medic needed on the command deck, medic needed on the command deck, code Teal," Hamza, spoke clearly into his earpiece.

Within seconds a team of nurses appeared and began tending to the Acting Secretary General.

"He's turning blue, clear the area!"

Hyrum Jeffs was now splayed unconscious on the floor of the command deck of UN Global Headquarters outside New York City.

"Starting chest compressions…"

Several minutes later, Hyrum Jeffs was in a comfortable chair, still on the command deck. His shirt was open, his bare chest exposed to the world. He was awake, but tired, drained of vitality, yet still in full command. The defibrillator marks on his chest tingled.

"Sir, I have news from China."

"Y-yes, Hamza, go ahead."

"Wait, here, inhale this first," a nurse cut in and handed Hyrum Jeffs a plump and vibrant red rose with gnarled gold filaments reaching up from between the petals.

"What is it?"

"It's a LoRose, sir, a rose infused with lorazepam. Simply insert your nose into the core, and inhale deeply."

Hyrum Jeffs regarded the hybrid plant with suspicion.

"It's ok, sir," Hamza reassured his boss.

Hyrum slowly brought the flower to his face and breathed deep. Comfort and relief enveloped him.

"Wow, that is nice."

"Great. Now, about the Chinese, sir."

"Yes, go ahead."

"They've killed the Russian diplomats. All of them. The Red Chinese army is moving in all directions. They're flooding their borders with soldiers, sir."

"Thank God for this rose…"

"Sir?"

"Oh, yeah, ok. Let's throw some interference their way via communications jamming and call the Japanese Imperial Army to action. Have them launch a full out barrage from the Yellow Sea. That should buy some time for the African war machine and the Tartarians."

"Right away, sir."

"And can I get some new clothes, please?"

A short Mexican man appeared not long after with a fresh set of clothing.

"Who the hell are you?"

"My name is Xavier Santa Maria De Las Rosas, sir."

"What a mouthful," Hyrum Jeffs wasted no time in changing into the fresh clothing.

"Sir, Xavier is our new go-fer. He signed up to be a peacekeeper not long after the blast in San Francisco."

"And he's already here? He'll be replacing Gerhardt then?"

"Yes, sir. Xavier moves very fast, which is why he was recommended to serve directly under you."

"Good," Hyrum Jeffs turned to face Xavier. "As long as you don't *steal* like Gerhardt did. It'll be nice to have someone who actually wants to be here for once."

"Sir, our intelligence has informed us of something called Project Phlea Circus; a clandestine program of prescription drug testing performed on US citizens, prisoners, in Colorado, by a Japanese pharmaceutical concern, the Takashinden Amplified Science Corporation. Apparently it's gone belly up."

"…What?"

"Yes, this is the classified project deceased Secretary Cairns was directly overseeing. There's also a connection to several European governments via Claudio Benvolio of Italy."

"What's happened to the prisoners? The staff?"

"We're sending a team of Soldats there now…"

Warren G. Harding Above Top Secret Correctional Facility

Outside Wareland, Colorado

Unity Day +1

The bright blue UN craft hovered to a stop outside of the black webbing that encased the secret detention facility.

It was very quiet.

Two battalions of elite UN Soldats marched around the grounds and met at the top like a pincer.

There was no one around.

Together, the two groups marched in through the main gates and began taking stock.

The vast rows of staff housing were silent.

The cricket pitches, bars, Director's Island, soccer fields, the PolyMatic Football field, and the laboratories were all devoid of human activity.

The ionic field was non-existent.

The Soldats now moved inside.

They were greeted by a faint air of burnt butter.

Windows were smashed.

Doors were broken.

Cells were empty.

They arrived at the cafetorium.

The doors were sealed shut.

"Blowing the doors! Stand clear!"

Kaboom.

The smoke ebbed and the horror came into focus.

A sprawling pile of charred bodies.

In the middle was a throne of some kind.

On it sat the charred corpse of Stanton Finch.

All the bodies were "pointed" at the throne.

The hardened Soldats progress was now hindered by the sheer volume of human husks.

"Call this in…"

A noise from above.

All sixty-four guns were aimed at the source of the disturbance.

Dr. Kenji Hirasawa, half-naked and crazed, emerged from his hiding place in a crow's nest overlooking the cafetorium. His skin was ashen and his eyes were bottomless pits. His fingernails were pocked and bore the hallmarks of necrophagia.

"Endo… Endo…" he rasped in between chuckles. The Soldats couldn't see the half-eaten, rotting, corpse of Yoshida Endo at Kenji's feet. "Endo… Endo…"

"Is it all he can say?"

"What does it mean?"

"Hell if I know, bag 'im, tag 'im, and let's ship out. This place is going to haunt me for some time…"

Welcome to Our Amplified Earth

Depending on whose side you were on, the UN War of Consolidation, or the UN Unity Wars, dragged on for seven years.

The Great Abdication took place on 21 July 2115. The world gathered around television sets and holographic projection units to watch, one by one, their world leaders bow and swear allegiance to the United Nations and Acting Secretary General Hyrum Jeffs.

China remains hostile towards global unification efforts and has become a haven for all others also opposed.

Africa remains split down the middle. Any nations not already housing UN Peacekeepers turned and made sure to deport any UN loyalists and massacred any who opposed. More Chinese troops arrived by sea on the west coast to secure any nation who requested help, in spite of the Congolese war machine that stalked the eastern African seaboard.

For security reasons, UN Global Headquarters, or the UNGHQ, has become permanently mobile. The newly formed Extraordinary Council of Human Governance remains airborne on a stealth jet 20 hours a day, guarded by jets and ground support. The stealth craft lands to refuel and conduct business with diplomats in New York, London, Brussels, Ankara, Samarkand, Kolkata, Bangkok,

Manila, Buenos Aires, Vladivostok, Dar es Salaam, Canberra, and Tokyo.

Acting-Secretary General Hyrum Jeffs was made full Secretary General following his handling of the implementation of Article 939, the dissolution of the United States, the eradication of the Oil Pest, and his negotiations with the Scottish. However, Hyrum chose to serve under a pseudonym: Lewis B. Crofts. His growing paranoia and failing health led him to conceal his true identity from the record books. Hyrum Jeffs, together with Xavier Santa Maria De Las Rosas, disappeared into the froth of a new world shortly after the fighting stopped in 2122. Lewis B. Crofts, though, had a statue erected, a public holiday declared in his name, and an eternal flame lit in his honor, all following his sudden and untimely 'death' immediately following the end of the War.

The Scottish made their way to Vietnam and shocked the world with their effectiveness. In less than two years of heavy fighting, the country fell to Angus McDuff and his brave kilted warriors. A new port was established, and the country enjoyed a new renaissance. The people of Vietnam reacted favorably to UN ascension, largely due to the Scottish army's gentle and heroic disposition towards the locals. Very few personal homes and businesses were damaged, and during the reconstruction, the new ScotchViet government waived all taxes. The soldiers became builders, lifting Vietnam to a new found glory. By the end of the war, tartan patterns and bagpipes could be found in almost any home.

In Nagoya, during the war, professor Susumu Mitsune debuted his radical new radiation cleaning process. The nation-state of San Francisco contacted the professor and flew him over to heal their city and region. The clean-up took as long as the war itself, but when the task was complete, the region was completely radiation free. For payment, the professor asked that his family be allowed to relocate to San Francisco. They were granted this, where they immediately entered politics and took over the nation-state within several years. Thus the Mitsune Era of San Francisco began. With the United States being no more, the Japanese government sent an emissary over to Governor Iwao Mitsune in 2129. By 2131, San Francisco was renamed to San Fu-Kuo, and was governed by a vassal shogun, loyal to Tokyo and its interests. The UN ECHG allowed this in the spirit of new arrangements, and because Japan had proved instrumental in the success of the UN's war.

The armistice with China remains in effect. UN Peacekeepers daily patrol the border, while Chinese troops stand at the ready. There is a Demilitarized Zone in Hong Kong. Here, the UN's diplomatic wing maintains a permanent office for conducting trade and permanent ceasefire negotiations.

The single most influential change implemented by the UN was most likely the global legalization of all narcotics, drugs, and illegal substances. A single man in Mexico City was tasked with overseeing the proliferation and global distribution of hybridized drug-plants. Xavier Santa Maria De La Rosas had reemerged in the years following the war and his disappearance. His strange and aggressively covert new ideas for microfarming revolutionized food and drug production across the

Americas. Almost overnight Xavier El Burro established himself as the world kingpin of narcoplants. Although his precise methods are classified, the volume, quality, and logistics of his product justified any level of secrecy.

With no central government, large cities in the former United States reorganized into nation states. The wealthiest members of each locale pooled their monies to ensure the infrastructure and ways of life were maintained until the UN could send in armed Democracy Squads to firmly establish local, loyal, governments. Chicago became Chicagoland. Los Angeles became the Capitalist Empire of Los Angeles. The extremely wealthy in Palos Verdes, Malibu, and Beverly Hills began work on isolating themselves from the rest of world by means of a force field dome. Texas declared itself a sovereign nation once more. New York City renamed itself as New Amsterdam, Incorporated. Sadly, the middle of the United States devolved into a semi-permanent war zone. Cross-country travel by land through this section of the continent became very dangerous, very quickly. UN troops patrolled the region, but the locals proudly defended their portions of land from anyone and anything that they didn't immediately recognize.

Aside from the commotion and general anarchy of the Great Plains, the other Nation States of the former United States thrived under UN rule. Cultures blended with an air of loving cohesion. Each new UN Global Citizen managed to make room for the other.

In time, China ordered half of their army to stand down, but still refused full cooperation with the UN and its members.

There are no passports.
There are no borders.
There is only free trade.
There is only The UN.

Timeline

Sunday, January 1, 2113

Svalbard Incident
(Chinese Oil Catastrophe)

July 2113

The Crush begins

November 2113

Inception of WGH Prison concept.

March 2114

Construction of WGH is begins.

November 2114

United States Election.
Construction of WGH completed.
Prisoner transfer begins.

Tuesday, January 1, 2115

Warren G. Harding Above-Top-Secret Federal Penitentiary opens.

Saturday, March 23 2115

Alcatraz Island is sloppily resurrected, staffed, and glutted with European prisoners.

Sunday, July 14, 2115

Kaboom

Monday, July 15, 2115

Unity Day

www.ingramcontent.com/pod-product-compliance
Lightning Source LLC
LaVergne TN
LVHW010649110826
845149LV00014B/3010

* 9 7 8 1 9 5 7 1 7 4 0 3 7 *